THE
LATE SHIFT
Specialist

for Trevor & Sally
— some thoughts from the heart
Hope you enjoy!

best wishes,

Alex Dunlevy

January, 2022

THE LATE SHIFT SPECIALIST
Copyright © 2020 Alex Dunlevy
The moral right of the author has been asserted.
www.alexdunlevy.com

Typesetting and cover design by Formatting Experts

ISBN 978-1-8382227-2-7
Published by Volker-Larwin Publishing

THE
LATE SHIFT
Specialist

A COLLECTION
OF SHORT STORIES

ALEX DUNLEVY

STORIES

THE SECRETIVE MAN

I don't know a lot about my Dad. Partly that's because he's not been around for the last fifty years to tell me anything, but it's also because he was that kind of man – the sort that can't give freely of themselves – so you'd have to probe to find out anything at all. And I wasn't big on probing when I was fourteen.

At forty-five, Alec was old to become a Dad, so I suppose there was a fashionable *generation gap* between us. To me, this was more about not getting to kick a ball around with my Dad like other kids could with theirs, or the hot-faced embarrassment felt on sports days or speech days when some school friend would ask, in shocked tones, "Is that your Dad, the old bloke with the white hair?" It certainly didn't lead to any James Dean-like, angst-ridden failure to communicate on our parts, though as a family we were never good at just coming out and saying things as they really are; too British, perhaps.

Alec was born an unbelievably long time ago, in 1908, so I guess even the Great War must have left some impressions on him that I failed to extract. In truth, I know very little about his early life, but I do know that he was a physical chap with a good brain. Whilst at university, each week he would cycle from home in Horsham,

Sussex, to Birkbeck College in London, where he read history. Proud of his powerful physique, and strikingly handsome with wheat-gold hair and blue-grey eyes, he soon developed the ability to charm. He would have held forth over a few pints at The Dog and Bacon in Horsham with a circle of friends and adoring barmaids. On other days he might have strolled round Warnham Mill Pond with an early love and talked about an uncertain future with the Jarrow March a recent memory and the Great Depression looming.

Difficult times, for sure, but I see him, in those days, crossing the Downs in an open-topped car, perhaps a Morris Eight Tourer, blond hair and university scarf flying carefree in the breeze, a couple of drinking chums in the back and a full-lipped, almond-eyed girl by his side (the type that always featured in his casual doodles). He has a quizzical, lop-sided smile on his face whenever he looks at her. Sometimes he's shouting and half-turning his head to be heard over the noise of the engine. The chums are nodding and laughing while she smiles indulgently, captivated by his roguish charm.

His favourite American actor, Alan Ladd, with an excruciating English accent and standing on a small soapbox, plays the romantic lead in this version of Dad's early life. Sophia Loren is by his side, and the chums are taken from the cast of Doctor in the House. The words *bounder*, *cad* and *absolute rotter* feature regularly in the screenplay.

By the time Hitler got around to invading Poland, Dad was already thirty-one. At that age he was spared combat duty and spent most of the war in Coastal Command. Towards the end of that time, as the war was ending in Europe, there was a passionate affair with a WAAF called Olive which we would discover, sixty years later, had resulted in a secret child.

After the war, Alec decided to put that physique to good use and went to study physical education at Loughborough. Still on the rebound from Olive, he met a twenty-three-year-old ex-WAAF from Lancashire called Sadie. She had stepped out of one of his drawings with her full red lips, green eyes and long, wavy black hair – more Rita Hayworth than Sophia, perhaps – but definitely in the genre. In a few short months and aided by a couple of adjustments to the facts, his charm did the trick and they were married in early 1947.

He had told Sadie that he was seven years younger than he was and omitted to mention Olive or their baby. To me, this says almost as much about Sadie's famous convent-school naïveté and gullibility as it does about Alec's vanity and readiness to deceive. As was bound to happen, the stupid age lie was discovered at a family event a few months later but my mother knew nothing about Olive or the child (David) until she was eighty-three years old.

Dad had carried his secret to the grave almost forty years before.

THE CHINAMAN'S DOG

Up and out. Every other day. That's the only way. For The Runner is a hearty boy in the morning. No time for resolve-draining preliminaries or precautions. He wakes with the pavement hitting the feet, the body tightening. Calves, buttocks, stomach, testicles tightening with the rhythmic thud. Gradually, head and eyes clearing.

As he runs, he says hello to every one of the few people he passes and tries an encouraging smile. It's a policy decision. A small but stubborn investment of goodwill, despite the disappointing returns. At least half the people ignore him. He forgives them, knows most of them are self-absorbed or half-asleep or frightened of strangers. Others clearly regard him as deranged. Some mumble uncomfortably, but hooray: one in five or so responds with a cheery "Hello" or a friendly "Hi" or even a "Beautiful morning isn't it?" These he adopts as his *regulars* and he often thinks about them.

Down the hill, past the multi-coloured terraced-houses he runs to the dawn-lit cemetery with the broken tombstones, the forgotten, untended graves, the litter and the graffiti, where the one-armed, winged angel stares out over the God-forsaken town.

He crosses the busy road to the haven of the canal, mist rising over the grey-green water. Swans glide,

5

mutely. A moorhen on tentative legs enters the water and upends itself in a momentary flash of white. Mallards hurry pragmatically along the water. Further along, a grey heron is still as a ghost on the far bank.

Breathing more laboured now, The Runner climbs up by the Victorian bridge to the disused railway track. Suddenly the sun breaks through and the joyous song of a skylark soars above the white noise rushing headlong from the motorway below. This is the unrelenting, uphill stretch now, a wide mud and cinders path along a woodland ridge with a grassy meadow sloping down to the right, where new housing has filled the valley below. In the distance, the chalk downs rise up and sunlight glints from abandoned hangars at the small aerodrome.

As he runs, The Runner is thinking of one particular regular: The Chinaman. He sees him most mornings along the railway. The Chinaman always acknowledges him with a nod and a smile that creases his already rumpled, brown face. Alone with his little dog, he is a man of perhaps sixty in a pale grey, nylon zipper-jacket. The Runner can see that he is alone, an outsider in his adopted country, carelessly ignored by cold, glass-brittle Englishmen. He imagines his sad life: the modest little house he struggles to keep clean, the lowly job at the factory or in the kitchens at the Chinese restaurant. There will be evenings when he cries for his long-dead wife, seeks compensation in bachelor routines and television shows he doesn't fully understand, comforted as always by the little dog at his feet.

As if summoned by his thoughts, at that very moment

the shuffling form of The Chinaman comes into view further down the track. The Runner resolves to be especially friendly on this glorious morning. Then, as the distance between them thuds away, he sees that The Chinaman is even more alone than usual.

"No dog, today?" he calls out, with what he hopes is cheerful bonhomie balanced with a decent amount of concern.

"Don' haf doah," says The Chinaman.

The Runner slows to a walk and stops, facing him.

"Yes. A *little* dog – what is he, a Scottie or a Schnauzer or something? Not a young dog, for sure, but a sweet, little chap. Where is *he* today?"

The Runner is aware that his voice sounds a little suspicious, accusatory even.

"Don' haf doah" says The Chinaman again, more definitely, then: "Men' yea' ago, haf doah bu' he die. Now no doah." A pause. "Men' yea' no doah."

The Runner knows he is on the verge of seeming ridiculous. Is he remembering something from many years ago? Does he have the wrong Chinaman? But he has no other Chinese regulars, cannot recall ever seeing another Chinese person on the circuit, in fact.

Groping for salvation, he blurts out:

"Well, maybe you should get another dog, then? Maybe it's time."

The Chinaman looks puzzled: "Maybe …"

The Runner attempts a twisted smile and then escapes by running off down the track. Sunlight is flashing through the trees like a strobe. *Am I losing it?* he thinks to himself. *I can picture that little dog. All those times I thought I saw him! They looked so right together.*

On and on he runs, up from the railway and into the town's beautiful gardens, past the aviary, the rows of dedicated benches, the rotunda and the giant beech trees, to the rose garden and the sundial with the missing gnomon and, as he runs, he tries in vain to forget about the strange and foolish encounter.

*

The front door of The Old Bakery closes, and Doctor Chang stands, wiping his feet on the mat. His pretty, young wife smiles at him and they speak in Cantonese.

"Nice walk, honey?" she asks.

"Yes. It's turning into a lovely morning. Funny thing, that lonely English guy spoke to me today."

"The runner? The one you feel sorry for?"

"Yes. He thinks my dog has disappeared."

"What dog is that?"

"I have no idea." He stares at her blankly.

"Perhaps he thinks you ate it with some yellow beans and a little rice wine?" She sucks in air through her teeth in an impression of Hannibal Lecter. Her eyes dance and she giggles as she hugs him gently.

PARADISE

It had been a bright, crisp, October day but now it was getting dark, turning chilly. The fog, or perhaps it was a river mist, made the taxi lights and the blue neon of the tube sign glow iridescent in the gloom. Friday night, and so busy earlier with the great surge of commuters swarming like flies heading south, but now that had slowed to a trickle of late workers, silently scurrying home with their briefcases, scrupulously avoiding eye contact. Amongst them were small groups of loud talkers, ties loosened, heading home plump from the pubs with faces like shiny, red apples.

Terry dodged behind a pillar when he saw her. She was wearing a suede coat again; almost an Afghan but neater, smarter, certainly more expensive. And with dark, brown boots this time. Forty years on, but he'd already known how she would look; she was back in the news. Eyes not quite so bright now, hair mousy rather than blonde and a little straggly. She was thinner too, perhaps, but God, she was still beautiful. Sixty-seven years old and she still had it, no question: those cheekbones, those full, sensuous lips.

He watched her unchanging mannerisms: the toss of the head to flick the hair away from her eyes, the tuck behind the left ear, the pulling up of the coat collar. And then, opening the compact for the cursory make-up check, the nervous look at her watch verified by a glance at the big station clock. Lastly, she tugged on her gloves and she was ready. It was six thirty-five.

Terry slipped out from behind the pillar and went up to her. She turned and gave him that radiant, teasing smile that had melted his heart, every time.

"You are late."

"Do you mean the five minutes – or the forty years?"

"Is it that long? My God!"

"It's 2008 now. Hadn't you noticed?"

She chuckled and squeezed his arm.

"I can't believe you wanted to meet here, you senti-mental old fool."

"I know, but why not? It was our weekly thing, after all. So, let's walk."

The dark sky was streaked with magenta and the sun was setting in a blue, yellow and crimson blaze that would have inspired Turner. He took her hand and they strolled across the bridge, feeling the weight of the great river beneath them, rolling into the night.

"You always preferred the other side," said Terry.

"It just felt safer, somehow."

"Well, south of the river was a bit rough in those days. So was I, for that matter."

"Rough? You and Maurice liked to think so. You were from the wrong side of the tracks, no doubt about that, but very sweet and charming. And gorgeous, of course."

"It's a while since anyone called him Maurice."

"Hmmm. Did all right, didn't he?"

"We all did, didn't we, in the end?"

"I suppose we did."

There was a companionable pause as they walked on, each reflecting on their lives and the many intervening years.

"So, what was it you wanted to tell me, Terry?"

She caught his arm and they came to a stop. He turned those deep, passionate, blue eyes on her.

"It's all over with Liz, Julie. She's gone back to Australia."

"Oh, you poor sod. You wait until you're sixty-four to get married and then it's all over in, what, four years?"

"Nearly five. It was all my fault," he added, heavily, and stared out over the black water. "I had this late urge to be a Dad. Not sure where it came from. Maybe it was knowing my own father was close to death, some instinctive urge to rebuild the family? I don't know. And then I met Lizzie. She was vivacious, young and strong. Thought she'd be good for me. So, I married her. Expected that we'd have kids and that she'd be my best friend as well as my lover, after a while. But it doesn't work like that, does it? The kids didn't materialise and, in the end, I guess the buggers were right; thirty-five years is just too big a gap. She could never relate to my memories. And I have so many memories. The past is all I have now, really."

"Oh, what rot! You total fraud, Terry! You're not that old, you're still really good-looking – if you would ever smile, that is – AND you're still working. All the bloody time, it seems! You have everything, in fact."

"Except someone to share it with."

"Come on grumps, let's keep walking. We might find one of our old pubs."

They linked arms and moved away from the bridge and through Parliament Square.

"And *you're* working again – and how! I had a sneak preview. It's bloody wonderful, Julie. Tragic, actually. You were *so* good. Almost too believable. You'll be off to LA again, I shouldn't wonder."

"Nominated, perhaps, but they never give it to old dears like me."

The dark, old pub was all brown wood and coloured glass, the bar area busy and shouty. They bought drinks and took a corner table, away from the crowd.

"You must have thought I was an idiot to get married," said Terry. "What was it you said that time?"

"I said: 'I've never quite understood why people get married.'"

"Yes – but then what did you call it – an artificial arrangement or something?"

"I said: *it was just an invented structure*."

"Maybe you were right."

Julie fell silent and toyed with the olive on a cocktail stick in her glass. Eventually, she looked up:

"There's something I have to tell you too, Terry."

"Go on."

She slipped off the exquisite, pale pink leather gloves and something caught the light. Terry felt like he'd been punched in the heart.

"It took me twenty-eight years, but Duncan and I were married last November, in India."

"I hadn't heard," he managed to whisper.

"No. I guessed you hadn't. It was a quiet wedding. We tried hard to keep it from the press."

She took his hand in both of hers and looked into his eyes.

"I didn't really change my views on marriage, Terry. But making that movie really affected us both. Suddenly, we wanted to be *sure* that we'd be there for each other. Do you understand?"

"Of course, I do."

Later, as they walked back, she said: "You have your work and such lovely friends, Terry. They all adore you; you're really very lucky."

"I know. But I was remembering you and me, back then. We didn't need friends, did we?"

He waved his arm at the lights of the South Bank, reflected in the dark river.

"We had each other, and we had all this. *This* was our *paradise*."

"It was a long time ago, Terry," she said.

Over to the west, the sun had quietly set, and the colours had drained from the sky.

THE GARAGE JOB

The job came through old friend Paul, who was already working there. It was to man the Esso pumps at weekends, run the little shop and answer a phone that never rang. It was an absolute doddle and quite lucrative with the added scams, according to Paul. Kit would do mostly Saturdays; Paul the long, lonely Sundays.

Saturdays, the guys were there all morning. The manager, Carl Silver, was a rumple-faced, Jewish man of about forty, always smiling. Dodgy? Probably yes, but in a kind way. He seemed to care about his family and would often bring his plump and useless twelve-year-old son Aaron into work, where he messed up the takings and ate all the sweets. His chief mechanic, Dick Ripley, was a shorter, more pugnacious character – good-looking but flash with it and uppity. You'd want to count your fingers after shaking hands with him.

Each drove a 3.8 litre Jaguar Mark II and sometimes they raced each other dangerously through the Buckinghamshire lanes. Meanwhile, the barely recognisable hulk of an XK-150 DHC lay rusting to the side of the garage. They said it was valuable and they dreamt of restoring it one day, but, to Kit, it looked like a heap of scrap.

It was always fun when they were around. Kit filled fuel tanks, checked oil, measured out Green Shield

Stamps and occasionally sold some windscreen wipers or a car mat. Carl would be smarming some hapless customer and wringing his hands like Uriah Heep while Dick was under the ramp in his baby-blue overalls, bashing metal and singing something lewd or wiping his hands on a rag and shaking his head as another expensive repair was sadly inevitable.

One of those repairs was occasioned by Kit on the day he managed to fill both tanks of an XJ12 with an enormous quantity of diesel, not petrol. A scintilla of doubt formed in his mind as the car left the forecourt and it grew over the following hour to a dread certainty, confirmed when the car limped back, trailing black smoke and backfiring, the driver fuming at his idiocy. Kit was surprised not to be killed, or at least fired on the spot, and kept a low and grateful profile for the rest of the day while Dick gave him withering looks every time he flushed more petrol through the stricken beast. But they did not even dock his wages.

The workshop always closed by two at the latest, the Jaguars raced away and then Kit would work alone until the seven pm closing time. It was quiet on those hot, lonely, summer afternoons. Between customers, he would read snatches of his French A-Level texts.

The job was well-enough paid, really, but Paul had shown him how to *augment* his income. There were the tips, of course, and Kit found himself studying customer-types and switching styles between matey, politely helpful and obsequious in his efforts to win greater rewards. He found that a liberal allocation of green stamps usually led to a larger tip and he made sure that the customers knew he was doing them a special favour. It was astonishing how a few lousy, extra stamps could lead to quite a large tip, often given with a conspiratorial wink. Pathetic. Also, he would always offer to clean the windscreen and check the oil. The women always went for this but then they would make him do the tyre pressures as well, which was a pain, and then tip him a feeble five pence like it was a crock of gold. The men were more generous, always, and understood that you had to tip anything, over and above pouring petrol, and that anyway, it was only right to reward a polite, young man working hard to better himself.

His friend Paul ripped off the stamps to a massive extent, filching great sheets of the things and making up his own books to claim gifts but Kit couldn't be bothered with all that faffing around for a toaster or something. He preferred the shop-based scams.

The basic scam was simply to sell things from the shop without ringing them up. Of course, you would have to ring it up if the customer commented or they needed a till receipt but that was almost never and, if the till was open anyway, you would get away with it or you could ring up *no sale* once in a while just to get in. You would just pop the customer's money into the till, give them their change with a smile and pop it shut again. All very professional. And, when you next had the till open, you would remember to help yourself to what they had put in. Of course, you had to do this only with plentiful things where stock checks were less likely, and any losses could be put down to customer theft. One of the zillions of £2.99 rubber mats would be okay but the only baby chair at £39.95 would be asking for trouble.

Kit's favourite, shop-based scam was the oil. Every time he sold a gallon can of Duckham's or Castrol GTX, he would forget to ring it up on the till, then find a similar, empty can round the back, clean it up, bash out any dents and fill it glug by glug with SAE30 from the massive workshop tanks and then place it to fill the gap in the display. One day, Paul pointed out that Duckham's oil was, in fact, dark green whereas SAE30 was brown so, after that, he only dared risk the GTX, but then he sold more of that anyway. No-one ever complained about weaker performance, so Kit figured Castrol were even bigger scammers than him.

Somehow it seemed all right, par for the course, *expected* almost, to be ripping off these dodgy characters who were undoubtedly ripping off their own customers. It was as if his ingenuity would be admired, if discovered. Like a clever joke, well-told. They would all have a laugh about it, lovable rogues together. It never occurred to him that his kneecaps might be smashed with a baseball bat or some such horror.

But anyway, Kit needed the money. He wanted a car of his own. At his age that was essential if you wanted to ask girls out. And he made a principled point of never ripping off the customers by overcharging or short-changing them. That would clearly be wrong.

*

One Saturday afternoon in August, a petrol tanker drove up and the driver came into the shop.

"All right mate? Got eight hundred gallons for Carl. Okay to drop it down your tank?"

Kit didn't quite understand, and he noticed that a customer had just driven up to the pumps in a beige Volkswagen Beetle.

"Er ... I dunno. Carl didn't say anything."

"Well it's a regular arrangement we have. It's no problem."

"Look. Can I just serve this bloke?"

"Sorry, mate. Really can't hang about. And Carl will be seriously pissed off if he misses out on this."

Kit chewed his lip and stared anxiously at the driver.

"All right. Hang on. I'll call him."

As the phone was ringing, Kit worried about the guy waiting. Making customers wait this long was not the way to get himself a decent tip.

"Hello Kit. What's up, buddy?"

Kit explained the situation.

"I wasn't expecting him today and I'd rather be there, to be honest," said Carl, the irony of his chosen phrase passing him by. "But I guess it's okay. He gets fifteen pence a gallon. Have you got a hundred and twenty quid in the till?"

Kit checked.

"Just about, yeah."

"All right. Let him start pumping and I'll come right over."

The driver had overheard, gave a thumbs-up and headed outside. He swiftly brought the truck in, lifted the heavy, metal lid to the echoing, subterranean tanks and attached the fat, flexible pipes from the truck to the petrol tank. Kit heard the pumping start as he finally approached the customer.

"I'm awfully sorry to have kept you waiting, sir," he started.

The big man was stepping out of his car.

"It's all right, lad. I'm not in a hurry." He grinned, but his eyes were not smiling. "And I don't need petrol anyway. Just seemed like a good place from which to watch, actually. Perhaps we could talk in your shop?"

The man introduced himself as Gibson, Customs and Excise, Investigations.

Kit's heart froze. This would be the end of everything and there was no way of warning Carl now.

"I've been following this tanker for weeks. It's a common scam," Gibson said, looking bored with the whole thing. "The driver short-delivers his big customers where he can. That way, when he's finished all his deliveries for the week, he still has plenty of petrol on board. Then he drops the rest into a friendly tank and they split the money. Cash only. Easy money for him, half-price petrol for your boss to sell at a big profit."

"I had no idea."

"Lucky for you that you made that call, son. I assume the boss is on his way?"

"He'll be here in a few minutes."

"Righto. I'll just go and spoil the driver's day then. You might want to put the kettle on; some strong tea with lots of sugar?"

As the kettle boiled, Kit's eyes fell on his much-annotated copy of Camus' "La Peste."

Arrested before one's A-Levels; that would have been deeply shameful, he sniggered nervously to himself. And then he felt sad, suddenly very sad, for the real-life plague that was about to be visited upon the house of good-hearted Carl. It didn't seem fair, somehow.

THE BUTCHER OF CADENAS

Mallorca, 1936

On August the sixteenth, a force of some eight thousand Republican militia, led by Cuban poet and revolutionary Alberto Bayo, made a bold, amphibious landing on the east coast of Mallorca. Over the next eleven days, this mixture of idealists – communists, loyalists, anti-fascists, and anarchists – moved rapidly inland. But their initial success would not last. Italy's colourful, fascist leader Arconovaldo Bonaccorsi, known as *Count Rossi* on account of his imperious manner and his red beard, rapidly brought fresh supplies and crucial air support to the beleaguered Nationalists. By the end of August, the tide was turning firmly in their favour and, by September the twelfth, the rebels' bombers had been destroyed and the men driven off the island in a disorderly retreat. Mallorca was now under Nationalist control and occupied by the Italians. It would remain so for the rest of the Spanish war and beyond.

Now that the fighting was over, word went out that the communists should be punished for their audacity. Harsh reprisals were ordered by Rossi's *Dragones de la Muerte*.

*

Alfredo Masqueda was twenty-six and Mallorcan, born and bred. The war that had torn Spain in two, dividing villages

23

and families, had forced a stark choice on everyone: red or black. To him, it seemed that the shambolic and communist-leaning aspects of the Republican cause could only lead to anarchy so, as a natural conservative, he had opted for the seemingly lesser evil of the Nationalist blackshirts. Within a couple of years, he had found himself as a Lieutenant commanding a small platoon in his home town of Cadenas.

When the call for reprisals came, the Captain, who was from Valençia, called him to his office:

"The message is clear, Masqueda. We are to strike at the very heart of local communist sympathisers. I want you and your men to arrest the local workers' committee members right away and bring them here."

Eighteen members were forcibly rounded up, all young men under forty. Masqueda recognised most of them and had even been to school with some, but it had been made crystal clear what was expected of him. He straightened his uniform, closed his heart and ordered his men to tie them to posts. Then his men placed blindfolds over their eyes, though one man refused to wear his, Masqueda noticed. As soon as this was done, his instructions to the firing squad were swift and brutal: "Load … Aim … Fire! One to the right. Load … Aim … Fire! One to the right again. Load … Aim … Fire! … Stand down."

The smoke slowly dispersed after the deafening volleys. Broken bodies were slumped sideways or forwards, pulling against the retaining ropes. The hot silence was oppressive, broken only by the soft moans of the one man who had not been killed outright. A sickly, animal smell of freshly spilled blood pervaded the sultry air.

Despite their battle scars, every man there was deeply shocked. And now Masqueda had to administer the coup-de-gras with a pistol bullet to the back of each head. By the time he reached his old school friend, his hand was shaking, and he was in tears. Françisco looked up at him. He knew death was coming but there was love in his eyes.

"I forgive you, Alfredo" he said. Then, with an aching heart, Masqueda pulled the trigger once more. Later that evening, his sister Isabel was deeply upset too, but at last she managed to put his own thoughts into words:

"It's war, Alfredo; war that is evil. You are not an evil man. You chose your side and then you had no choice but to follow orders. I know that and I know you. But many in the village will not understand. You must leave now; tonight, before they come for you."

Mexico City, 1979

Rosa put down her mop and bucket and the yellow, plastic carrier full of cleaning agents and rang the bell. She did this only as a courtesy, because she kept a key in her housecoat. After half a minute, she concluded that the old man must be out, or sleeping it off again, so she opened the door.

It was the stench that hit her first, then the flies, then the sound of the rope straining and creaking faintly. Somehow, she knew that sound even before she forced herself to look up.

After they cut him down, the policeman spoke to her kindly:

"I'm sorry you had to see that, Rosa. Are you okay?" She was dabbing her eyes and nodding, knowing she would never be okay.

"What can you tell us about this man?"

Rosa explained that she knew him only as Carlos and believed him to be Spanish, not Mexican, and that he had lived here quietly for about seven years. He had been kind to her and always paid her on time.

"Do you know if he had any relatives, next of kin?"

"Not here. I never saw any relatives or even friends. He talked about a sister sometimes."

"And this – there is a Spanish postmark – can you tell me anything about this?"

He handed her a letter.

She read: BUTCHER! THE DEAD OF CADENAS REMEMBER YOU. It was carefully hand-printed. She turned the single sheet over. There was no signature. She took the envelope from the officer and noted the ninety peseta Spanish stamp and the Palma postmark. The address was also carefully printed and had no errors.

She paled visibly and looked at the officer, shaking her head in fright.

Mallorca, 1980

"Thank you so much for agreeing to see me," said the woman journalist.

"You'll have to excuse me. I don't have many visitors these days," said Isabel, making space for the coffee and a plate of her custard pastries before moving her knitting off the armchair and sitting down.

The journalist waited until she was settled then looked at her kindly and spoke softly.

"So, you must have been very upset to hear about Alfredo's death last year."

"Of course, I was, but I was not so surprised when they told me about the letter."

"I don't understand."

"I knew he was in Mexico. We still talked once in a while and exchanged the odd letter. He'd been there seven years and thought he was finally free of it. And then, of course, there was the amnesty."

"Amnesty?"

"Yes. Three years ago the Spanish government announced an amnesty. It was controversial here, but all crimes committed in the Franco era were pardoned."

"So, he took this as good news?"

"He was hopeful, yes. But you have to understand, by then his *whole life* had been consumed by guilt and paranoia. For him, there had been nothing else. A pardon was some kind of forgiveness for him. A glimpse of salvation. A life raft perhaps, or so he thought."

"Perhaps you could start from the beginning for me?"

"After the shootings, here in Cadenas in 1936, he left for Madrid that night and joined the militia there. He was still there when the first letter arrived, the following year."

"What did it say?"

"The same. Always the same: BUTCHER! THE DEAD OF CADENAS REMEMBER YOU' And, of course, Alfredo panicked. Thought they were coming to get him. Right away, he volunteered to serve on the Russian front. Nobody volunteers for this, you understand?"

The journalist looked steadily at her, nodding.

"The second letter arrived in Russia in 1942. He is in such a state that he gets himself badly wounded the very next day and is invalided out of the army. Eventually, he returns to Madrid, with a pronounced limp now, but manages to set himself up as a motor mechanic in a quiet street. I am proud of him. He seems to be coping, you know?"

"And the second letter was the same?"

"Always the same. Same words, same postmark, same printing. Everything exactly the same, always. Only the price of the stamp changes."

Isabel topped up their coffees and passed the cakes.

"I thought he was getting on quite well there but, in 1944, the third letter arrives and he goes to pieces. Tells me there is a revenge killer on his trail. Tells me he has to disappear completely. He starts running."

"Where did he go?"

"Africa of all places: Spanish Guinea. Equatorial Guinea I think they call it these days? A dump. Much worse then, before the oil. No money at all, outside the hands of a few crooked despots. And so hot! The only good thing about it was that they spoke Spanish. But Alfredo survived, for five years. Then, in 1949, the fourth letter arrived."

"How on earth did they find him there?"

"I have no idea. But they always found him, in the end. After that, he ran to Peru, then Cuba, then Nicaragua.

It was the same story. He'd feel safe for a few years but then a letter would arrive and he'd have to up sticks, leave everything and run again. Finally, after the seventh letter, he fled to Mexico City. That was in 1972. Last summer, after seven years without a letter, and with the amnesty, he was beginning to sound more positive, less paranoid. He was drinking less, thank God. He even suggested I might fly out to see him. We hadn't seen each other for over forty years. But then, when that eighth letter finally arrived, it must have destroyed all that hope in an instant. It must have been too much for him to bear."

She took a lace handkerchief out of the sleeve of her cardigan and dabbed her eyes.

"Someone in the village said that Françisco was your sweetheart."

"Oh no, no. He was a sweet, gentle boy but we were never lovers."

At the door, the journalist turned back.

"Thank you again, Isabel. Tell me. It's lovely here, but do you still manage to get into Palma? It's such a beautiful city, isn't it?"

"Oh, once in a while, dear. There's a very good bus service."

JACK AND THE DOGFISH

It's eleven am but The Hind's Head is dark until his eyes adjust. Wooden stalls divide booths with red leather seating. She is in a shaft of sunlight and dust motes.

"Hi Jack. Looking good."

"You too, Sue."

They hug gently; friends reunited.

"Hope you don't mind meeting here. At least it's private."

"It's fine."

They sit facing one another and order coffee. Sue is taking photos from her handbag.

"So, these are my gorgeous daughters …"

Jack watches her introduce photo after photo. She *does* look pretty good. But her hair is dyed blonde now and thicker. It's in that same, long style and that's not right for a woman of fifty-one. She's wearing too much make-up and some unpleasant, musky perfume. Her clothes look expensive, but flashy. She's become more Diana Dors than Doris Day, somehow. Nevertheless …

"No photos of your husband?"

"I didn't think you'd want those."

"What's he like?"

"Good-looking, tall and dark. Hmmm."

She seems to want to add caveats but changes tack instead.

"So, did *you* ever get married? Kids?"

"Got close a few times but I *struggle with commitment*, apparently. Had lots of *experience* though," he adds mischievously.

"Ha! That bloody word."

"You remember?"

"Are you kidding? It's haunted me for thirty-eight years."

Her eyes are dancing now, and the intervening years have vanished. Jack is back in Evelyn Avenue in 1967. Someone is calling him …

*

"Can I help you?" The man laid down his garden shears. "Only I keep seeing you passing, up and down this bloody road. Up and down like a whore's drawers, as they say." He grinned.

Jack's young face flushed. "I'm visiting someone."

"Did you forget the number?"

"No."

"Well then … oh, *I* get it. It's a girl."

"Mmm."

"House number?"

"Hundred and fifteen."

"Okay. Young Susan, then – right?"

Jack nodded, cringing inside.

"Okay, young fella. Let's go."

And the Irishman frog-marched Jack two houses down, to the front door.

"Go on then."

"What?"

"Don't give me *what*. Ring the bloody bell is what!"

"But *you're* here."

"All right. You've thirty seconds, then I'll ring it *for* you."

The neighbour withdrew, shutting the gate carefully.

"I'm watching," he called over the freshly clipped hedge.

A deep breath and Jack's heart pounded as he watched the miracle of his hand, inching up and finally pressing the doorbell. He was desperate to run away but the neighbour was watching and miming applause.

"All right, all RIGHT!" came an irritable voice from inside. Jack stepped back.

A man of fifty was staring over spectacle rims.

"Yes?"

"Is Sue in?"

The father looked him up and down.

"Susan? She might be. And you are?"

"I'm Jack; from primary school. I used to come here. We played Ludo, ate fairy cakes …"

*

Sue looked apologetic. Her hair was in a towel.

"Jack? Gosh. I haven't seen you in years."

Jack hesitated. She seemed so grown-up, so gorgeous.

"I – er – I just wanted to ask you out …"

She smiled, encouragingly.

"… to the pictures on Saturday?"

"What's on?"

"Thunderball; it's James Bond."

"Oh, I'd *love* to see that. But would *Sunday* work? I'm shopping on Saturday."

"Sure. Outside the cinema, at a quarter to two?"

"Okay. Want to come in?"

"I'll let you dry your hair. See you Sunday."

Jack was grinning idiotically, snaking back through the gate.

"Which one?" yelled Sue.

"What?"

"Which cinema?"

"Oh, sorry – the Astoria."

The neighbour gave a 'thumbs up' as he ran past. Jack wanted to turn a cartwheel, but he didn't know how.

*

The cinema looked quiet but then it was a sunny afternoon. As Jack approached, though, he saw the sign: *Doors Open 4.15*. His heart sank.

Sue wore a cardigan the colour of rich egg yolks over a white blouse and grey, pleated skirt. In the breeze, her Alice band struggled to restrain her long, fair hair. She smiled broadly and tucked some rogue strands behind her ears.

"I've messed up," he said, pulling a face. "The times are different on Sundays."

She looked at the sign. "Ah."

"I'm sorry; I thought it would be like Saturday."

"It's my fault for making you change the day."

"No, it's not." He smiled, ruefully. "But it's kind of

34

you to say that. Look, let's go back to my house. You can meet Mum and Dad and drink Mum's ginger beer."

*

Three hours later, the cinema lights dimmed, and Jack knew this was his cue to hold Sue's hand or put his arm round her. He felt nervous and waited for a tender moment in the film. Every few minutes he thought *maybe now?* but his arm wouldn't budge. The longer it went on, the more difficult it became. Sue glanced across once or twice but still he couldn't respond. When the film ended, he was close to tears.

Fresh air brought relief. They stood on the steps, just breathing, then Jack suggested fish and chips. Sue chose cod. Jack chose rock salmon. As they walked on, she said:

"It's not really salmon, you know."

"No?"

"It's dogfish."

"Is that bad?"

"No, it's just not salmon. It's a fraud. It's a little shark."

"Well it tastes good: creamy, soft, no bones."

They lapsed into silence.

By the railway, they followed stairs down to a copse where a path led to Evelyn Avenue. She laid a hand on his arm. It was their first touch.

"Listen, Jack. Thanks for asking me out. It's been nice. But I'm not going out with you again." She looked at him, searchingly, flitting from eye to eye, checking for damage. "And, honestly? Before you ask any more girls out, you need more experience."

"I should walk you home," he called after her, "at least."

"No. It's still light. I'll be fine."

A few moments later he heard shoes clacking on the wooden footbridge and she was gone.

He aimed a massive kick at a stone and caught it perfectly. It flew through the air and hit a tree, dead centre. The new pain in his foot seemed to offset the pain in his heart, somehow. He hobbled slowly home.

*

Sue is saying something: "I said you needed more "experience" but later I worried about how that had made *me* sound. What was I? Thirteen? And *so-oh* experienced? You must have thought I'd been at it since puberty!"

Jack had never thought that, but he laughs dutifully.

"I was mean. Didn't give you much of a chance."

"I was a hopeless case."

"You were young." She puts her hand on his thigh and her touch electrifies him. "But you weren't hopeless. Anyway, the next morning I knew I had to put things right."

"You did?" Jack is breathless with astonishment.

"I walked to your house, then up and down your road, hoping I'd see you. I wanted to ring the doorbell, but I just couldn't."

The revelation fills Jack with both excitement and despair.

"What would you have said?"

"Just that I wasn't *at all* experienced *either* and it had

36

been a stupid and hurtful thing to say and that I'd go out with you again, if you asked me."

"God. Things could have been so different. And you didn't think to write, afterwards?"

"I wrote letters. Tore them all up. Was convinced you'd hate me."

Outside, storm clouds are forming. Sue stops at a Mercedes sports car.

"Yours?"

"It was a gift from my husband for my fiftieth."

"Wow. Generous guy."

"He's got money," she says flatly.

They arrange to meet again, at Jack's local. Sue says lunch is easier as her husband will be at work.

*

Sue is running from the rain. She looks younger, somehow, more glamorous.

"Wet hair again?" he quips.

She pulls a face and tucks some strands behind her ears.

After ordering, they sit in the window seat, legs touching lightly.

"So, tell me about your husband. He's good-looking and massively generous but …?"

"He's Scottish. From a family of puritans. He's a senior manager at the airport."

Sue stares hard at her glass.

"Gordon's very controlling, Jack. I had to threaten to leave him before he'd let me get a job. He'd much rather

37

I stayed home, like a good, little wife. He won't let me go anywhere, do anything, *be anything*."

"What about those Caribbean cruises in the photos?"

"Oh, he *takes* me places. We go places as a family. But I'm talking about *me*. He allows me no freedom."

"Isn't freedom something you have to take?"

"He gets so angry, Jack. It frightens me."

"Is he violent?"

"He's never hit me, no, but he's a bully. He physically dominates me, shouts at me and then freezes me out. Once, he didn't speak to me for two weeks."

A tear trickles down her cheek and Jack has no difficulty, this time, in putting his arm around her and wiping the tear away. She looks up, her pale blue eyes wounded and entreating.

"I'm leaving him, Jack."

At this point, the food arrives, and they order another drink. They touch each other more freely as lunch progresses. There are more tears but laughter, too.

By late afternoon, they are in bed together at Jack's house. The drinks have taken away their inhibitions. Their lovemaking is gentle and intimate, then intensely passionate.

They lie back on the pillows.

"Wow. You sure found that experience."

He sits up, breathes deeply. An aircraft whines overhead then fades, leaving only birdsong and the patter of raindrops on the roof.

"So, you're leaving Gordon."

"Yes."

"Why haven't you left him already? It's been what, twenty-five years?"

"Twenty-seven. At first, I couldn't because of the girls."

"And later?"

"When the girls left, I started building my escape fund."

"And now?"

"Now I'm nearly there. He's been okay recently, though, and my job helps me feel better about things. And we have a very comfortable life: a big house in Bourne End. On my own, I'd struggle to get some crummy flat."

"And the lovely car."

"Yes, but all that comes with Gordon. Look, Jack, I know it's ridiculously early to suggest this …"

"Suggest what?"

"I could divorce Gordon and we could be together at last."

"Wow. Where would we live?"

"Well, I'd be happy to live *here*. Or we could get somewhere new together. I'd have the divorce proceeds – lots."

Jack looks shocked. Sue bites her lip.

"Maybe I shouldn't have said anything." She touches his arm. "It's just an idea. Give it some thought. Now I must go; Gordon's home soon. Okay?"

He nods but it isn't okay. It really isn't.

*

Afterwards, he thinks about the women he has loved. They were strong and independent. Sue is neither. She didn't find the courage, years ago, to ring that doorbell or send a letter. She married a hunter-gatherer who keeps her in his cave. Maybe Gordon killed her courage. Maybe she never had any. She hasn't escaped his bullying and probably never will without another safe and prosperous cave to run to. And she hadn't the moral strength to be true to him until she left. Jack knows that was his fault too, but that doesn't excuse her. They were *her* wedding vows not his, after all.

Eventually, Jack's eyes fill with hot, angry tears of disappointment. Things have come full circle.

At their next lunchtime, he is calm and cool.

"Look, I'll get straight to the point, Sue. Last week was nice but I don't think we should meet again. This time it's *you* who needs more experience; experience of *life*. You'll get that by finding the courage to leave Gordon and make a life *for yourself*, not by running from his cave to mine."

He stands up.

"If you really *want* to leave him, that is, and I'm not sure that you do. I'm not even sure that you should."

He puts a hand on her shoulder. She looks up like a frightened rabbit, but he knows that she'll take good care of herself. She always has.

TEA WITH MUM

She thought about it every time she went round. One day, she would press that button and there would be no answer. Come the day, she would calm herself. Mum just hadn't heard the bell. She had probably forgotten her hearing-aid again. She might have fallen asleep. And then Jen would use her key and let herself in.

*

It was almost five years now, since the divorce. She had found herself the victim of a cliché: the younger woman. But not only younger. This one was prettier, brainier and better off than Jen, and presumed to be fertile. And when they'd met – just the once – she seemed a nicer person than Jen, too; sweet, almost apologetic, kindly ignoring Jen's barbed and snide rejoinders. The bitch.

When they'd sold up and the lawyers had split the proceeds, Jen didn't have enough to stay in Richmond and there were too many memories there anyway. She decided to move down to Eastbourne, get a little place near Mum. Just for a while. Give her back some time. Help her out a bit. Get to know her again.

But it hadn't been wholly altruistic. When Jen was with Mum, she was forgiven. Life became simple again. Mum gave her perspective, reminded her of all Jen's little achievements, told her not to be so hard on herself. Told her life wasn't all about having a family. Said she'd never taken to Farouk anyway and Jen was well shot of him. More fool him. He'd lost a wonderful woman. And there were plenty more fish in the sea. Much nicer fish, it had to be said. She irritated the shit out of Jen sometimes but when Mum looked – really looked – into Jen's eyes, as she sometimes did, Jen saw such sweetness and gentleness there. Had there been a God, she would have got down on her knees and thanked Him for Mum and the unconditional nature of her love.

*

They got into the habit of meeting for tea, most days. Jen finished her new job at four and then it was just a short walk to the little house where Mum had lived for twenty-five years. She had made it a haven of comfort and neatness. But, inevitably, standards started to slip as the osteoporosis advanced. Jen would rummage through her cupboards and the back of the fridge to root out the ten-year-old spices and the forgotten jars with the mould inside. She did this when Mum was in the bathroom and popped them into a bag which she put outside. Later, she took the bag home to her own dustbin.

Every visit, they made tea together.

"Earl Grey for me," Jen reminded her, "and not too strong."

Mum took out her special china cups and saucers with a little jug for the milk. She always had cake or biscuits on matching side-plates with freshly ironed napkins for the crumbs. She asked Jen to carry the tray through. In the living-room, the TV would be show-ing some dire quiz show, usually on the channel with all the adverts.

"Have another piece, dear," she said. "Live a little." And Jen made a rueful face and acquiesced, despite the fake cream she loathed, and swallowed a second slice of the overly sweet cake. Mum always looked so pleased.

She was glad she had made the move. It had been good for them both.

*

Jen braced herself and used her key. She called out "Mu-um" in their familiar, sing-song way. It wouldn't do to shock her, not with that dodgy heart. Through the frosted glass in the door she saw the little bob of sil-ver-grey hair. That was good; she was in her usual chair.

It was tea-time but Mum was still in her pink dress-ing-gown. On the small side-table, her tea was half-drunk and there were dark, toast crumbs on her plate. It looked like she'd left her glasses upstairs again and was having to peer closely at the TV magazine, open on her lap. But she was wearing her glasses. She looked smaller, shrunken somehow, with her head slumped forward like that.

Jen fretted and paced around the room. She kept looking over at Mum as if expecting her to turn the page or suddenly look up and smile. But nothing changed. Nothing moved. The clock on the mantelpiece went on ticking.

She moved to the window and opened it. Out there, in that other world, life was grinding on relentlessly, ruthlessly unheeding. How dare the street look the same? Part of her wanted to rush out screaming, surround herself with shocked and sympathetic faces. But who would they be?

And then Jen *was* Mum for a few moments, looking out, quietly waiting for her daughter. Waiting for what passed by. Waiting for this day.

Jen turned and knelt and saw that Mum had ringed one of that night's programmes with a green highlighter. Then she took the cold arm in hers and felt for the pulse she knew she wouldn't find. There was a roaring in her ears and her heart was fluttering wildly but somehow, she reminded herself: she'd known this would happen.

She just hadn't expected it to be today … Not today.

TILT

Maybe *The Who*'s lyrics were somehow to blame? *Hope I die before I get old* and *That deaf, dumb and blind kid.* Certainly, it all started with a pinball machine, back in 1969. In the Tatler Café, watching the postman feed his wages into that hungry slot, willing the odds to ramp up while his mug of tea cooled and the ketchup congealed on his fatty, bacon sandwich.

Jimmy saw him pulling back and releasing the sprung handle with that hard-earned precision, gripping the sides of the machine, thumbs hovering over the buttons, swaying and swerving, flipping and nudging each silver ball. Lights flashed as they ricocheted from the chunging, pinging islands, ultimately to be swallowed by one of the numbered holes. Always the postman was trying to nudge just enough to make a winning line without triggering the dreaded *Tilt* message that would make him cry out as he lost.

Jimmy had never seen obsession before, and it thrilled him. Especially on those all too rare occasions when the lights lit up, the tinny 1812 overture theme rang out and the machine spewed forth its silver avalanche of glittering coins. He wanted the postman to pocket his winnings then and walk away. It was only much later that he understood why he never did.

*

For Jimmy, it was football pools, lotteries and the like for a while. He was destined to win big. At work, he persuaded colleagues to join a syndicate, then spent his evenings wrecking his eyesight, precisely measuring where to put the crosses for the Daily Mail £25,000 Spot-the-Ball competition. He knew with geometric certainty that at least one of the twenty entries had to be no more than one thirty-secondth of an inch from the centre of the ball but all he won was a string of 'target prizes' allowing another go for free. The bastards weren't going to let him win.

By now, he bet on most things: lunchtime pitch and putt; evening darts or cards; even silly pub games or the toss of a coin. It was the spice he added to all his sustenance.

*

He discovered the stock market in the mid-eighties or, rather, it discovered him. He had been exploring the idea and had signed up for a couple of magazines. Then a charming American happened to call him one day. He wanted to share the exciting news about a revolutionary bio-chemical product. The shares couldn't remain cheap for long and now was definitely the time to buy. He called again a couple of days later; time was running out. This was a once-in-a-lifetime opportunity to get in on the ground-floor and make it big. He was very persuasive. Jimmy acquiesced. But the man had been calling from a boiler room in Gibraltar. When Jimmy went looking for him, everything had vanished, along with Jimmy's five grand.

Determined to have his revenge on the world of finance, Jimmy became an active investor over the next few years. All his spare money fed a growing portfolio of equities. He devoured *Investors Chronicle* and the *Financial Times*. He bought hardware and rented software. His home office became a dealing room. He studied companies and charts, moving averages, crossover points. And he had his successes. By the advent of spread-betting, in the late-nineties, he considered himself a savvy investor.

His work had gone well, the portfolio well-fed for several years. He was managing his own pension fund, an ISA, a large share portfolio and the new spread-betting fund. When his job finally folded, the redundancy payment gave him even more to play with. He decided to become a professional investor, which was a euphemism for doing absolutely nothing else.

Things went well for a while. He boasted to people that he was a professional gambler, just to shock them, but it just frightened the women away. He would bet a hundred pounds per point on the FTSE100 index and then go to lunch – or even the cinema – and discover later that he was so many thousands richer or poorer. He spent more and more time hunched over the computers. He was becoming addicted to the bitter-sweet taste of his own adrenalin. He even developed repetitive strain injury from gripping the mouse so feverishly for so long.

After a while, Jimmy noticed that the joy of the good days was getting more short-lived while the anguish of holding losing positions was deepening. He didn't know why.

He had always enjoyed a drink, so now he took to drinking more on losing days. It helped to deaden the pain. At first, he tried to avoid drinking before the UK markets closed, at four thirty pm. That would be unprofessional, after all. But soon he was drinking after lunch and, on really bad days, he would even *start* with a shot of something, just to get him going. Some days he would trade late into the night, following the American and Japanese markets with an ever-present whisky.

The spread-betting wasn't working out, but he tried different strategies and theories. He needed to get it right. The other funds had been doing okay with very little attention.

The Volatility Index (also known as The Vix or The Fear Index) had been livelier in 2007 but the crash came the following year. Jimmy had never seen the numbers fall so quickly. Like a one-armed bandit or a stopwatch in reverse. The pit in his stomach took up permanent residence. His equity funds collapsed. He sold out at the bottom and fed what was left into his spread-betting fund to benefit from the inevitable recovery. Eventually, he learned that recoveries are by no means inevitable in the timeframe you can afford and that the market doesn't care if you die waiting. It is supremely indifferent, in fact.

In the end, he had to sell the house to clear most of the debts and, by 2010, he was on the streets; bankrupt and unemployable, addicted to both alcohol and gambling. The market was recovering strongly by then, he read in the stray newspapers he found.

*

For two years he slept in shop doorways or under bridges. He fought for his turf, dodged the police, begged and stole. What money he scrounged went on booze. His smart clothes became filthy rags. A few of his teeth fell out. Most people ignored him. Those that did not, looked at him as if he were dog shit in human form.

Strangely, it felt right, somehow. Like this was where he was supposed to be. Perhaps he had always known he was worthless, deep-down, no matter what they said. He did not deserve to win – or even own – anything. He had set out on a very deliberate, subconscious path to self-destruction, or so his psychotherapist would say, later.

They had a few goes at saving him then, but there was always some sanctimonious prick that would try to bring Jesus into play. He had never been religious, and he resented being expected to sell his soul for their help. He was not that desperate; he would cope.

In the hospital, they said they could operate. The liver is a remarkable organ. It can grow back, apparently. He could not do much after the operation. He had been through the DTs before it and, of course, he could not get a drink in the hospital after it. A kind, young doctor suggested a course of rehabilitation:

"You're not old, Mr Wild, and you've done all the hard work of drying out," he said. "You could put this episode behind you now and find a full and happy life."

"Episode?" Jimmy said. "It feels more like the final chapter of a saga. One that was never going to end well."

"But it's your life, Jimmy. And you are the author of

the saga, remember? So, re-write the ending. Why not give it a try?"

"Yeah. Maybe I will, just for you, Doc. But I'm not placing any bets."

*

A few weeks later, he was out of bed and sitting quietly on the couch at the rehabilitation centre. No-one had mentioned Jesus, thank God; it was all cognitive behavioural therapy and taking back control. Jimmy was sorting himself out.

"Tea or coffee?"

He noticed that the orderly with the trolley was a different guy, older.

"Coffee, thanks. Milk, no sugar."

Jimmy looked him over as he carefully filled the mug. Saw the honey-coloured beard and the kindly eyes reflected in the gleaming hot water cylinder. There was something vaguely familiar; something from long ago. An aura, a fatherliness, a calmness of extraordinary depth. The guy was smiling beatifically as he brought the steaming mug over.

"Haven't we met before?" Jimmy tried to ask.

But the lights were getting brighter. Ridiculously bright. Was something going wrong with the power? It was blinding, suddenly, and Jimmy felt an odd weightlessness, but there was no noise apart from the blood roaring in his ears and then a warm and gentle voice:

"You know we have, Jimmy. I'm here to take you back."

REFERENDUM WAKE

Doug spotted more black ties on the other side of the bar and went over. Scarz was already halfway through a pint.

"What'll you have, mate? Mick's put a bit behind the bar."

"Oh, Stella – just a half, thanks."

"Half a quart of wifebeater for the boy, Jim," said Scarz.

"Well, here's to Mick," pronounced Doug, raising his larger than expected glass, "a good friend, a sensitive and intelligent chap with an enquiring mind and a great sense of humour."

"Well, I'll drink to that," said Scarz taking a gulp and wiping his beard with the back of his hand, "but that was twenty years ago, mate. The Mick of late (or should I say the *late* Mick?) was a grumpy old fart with an undue fondness for this stuff." He nodded towards the beers. "He fucking *lived* here – or in that hovel of his, surrounded by empties, chewing on bloody roll-ups and staring at the neon-God like he was hypnotised. Wept at all the bad news, the poor bugger."

"Yes. I did hear something about that," said Doug quietly. "Poor old Mick …"

They sipped contemplatively for a few moments.

"… And I remember his house was quite nice, thirty years ago. And then didn't his aunt leave him some place in France? What happened to that?"

51

"Yep. Dunno. Sold to pay for the booze, shouldn't wonder."

Doug looked at Scarz. Beneath the leather jacket was an AC/DC tee shirt stretched by a substantial beer gut. His hair was long and streaked with grey, the beard unkempt. There was a golden earring in his left ear and a tattoo of a motorbike on his forearm. His eyes were rheumy and his battered face had an unhealthy, dark pink sheen.

"Still got a bike?" asked Doug.

"'Course. Two actually. Despite this." And here he whacked his left leg. "Goldwing and an old Norton Commando. What about you – not still that fucking Lambretta, I hope?"

"No. Long gone. Four wheels for me these days."

Scarz ordered more beers, overruling Doug's protests.

"What a sight you were, though," he laughed. "The whole fucking kit: the parka with the Union Flag on the back, the dinky little haircut, the eight-foot aerial with the silly little pennant on it and about twenty fucking mirrors. What a twat!"

"At least we were doing something new! Looking different, listening to new music. And clean. Not like you bloody greasers – stuck in the fifties with your filthy old leathers and your Gene Vincent records."

Scarz punched him gently and then put his arm around him and they both chuckled.

"What did you do to the leg, anyway?" asked Doug.

"Replaced it." Doug's jaw dropped. "Had to. Some Tory voter in a fucking four-by-four made a nasty mess of the old one. Pulled out right in front of me, the bastard."

"And you're still riding?" Doug asked, in awe.

"Wasn't my fault, was it, so why stop? Just one of those things. Got used to the leg now and the wife seems to quite like it, bizarrely."

"So, I heard you married Jules?"

"You're well up to date, then. That was twenty-eight years ago, for Christ's sake! We're still together, mind. Had a couple of daughters. Long gone to their pathetic husbands. We're still here, though. Fat slobs now. No jobs, no prospects. Even lost the house. We rent a place now."

"Sorry to hear that." There was a pause. Doug tried to look sympathetic rather than appalled. "Still, Jules was a cracker though."

"Was until she married me. All downhill from there. You married?"

"Living with wife number three now, in Surrey."

"What happened to one and two?"

"I screwed up, frankly. Too many opportunities to play around. So, I did. Didn't go down well. Cost me a bloody fortune."

"Kids?"

"Yep. Two boys from number two plus Claire and I have a nine-year-old, Lucy."

Scarz looked at Doug, as if for the first time. He saw the trim figure, the lightly tanned face and the well-groomed silver hair, the expensive, dark suit.

"Bloody hell, a young wife too. You've done alright for yourself then. You're *looking* pretty good too, you old tosser."

Doug grinned. "Yeah. Just got lucky, really. Moved into IT in the late eighties. Turned into a good move. Contracting abroad for many years; good money."

"Hmm. Sounds like *you're* one of them Tory voters now then?"

Doug looked sheepish and quickly changed the subject.

"Talking of voting, what about tonight? I guess *you'll* be voting to leave, Scarz?"

"You'd guess right, mate. I don't know why we joined up with that lot in the first place. I mean, we've always hated the bloody French. Fought them for a hundred years. Fought the Krauts in two World Wars. And we've got zippo in common with those oily Mediterranean layabouts. It just made no sense. And then they go and invite all the rubbish from Eastern Europe to scrounge off the rest of us! And Turkey next? I ask you. Damned right I'm voting OUT, and good riddance."

"We're not what we were though, are we? As a country, I mean. Can we really survive without them?"

"We'll be fine. Actually, the question is, can they survive without us? If we leave, the whole shebang could go tits up. Plenty of other countries are having big doubts and moving to the right and the Euro's doomed, if you ask me. You can't share a currency without a unified tax and banking system; it just don't work."

Doug looked at Scarz with a new respect. Jim brought more beers, saying "the float's getting low now, lads; thought you'd appreciate a top-up".

"Cheers, Jim," they chorused. Some of the other guests were leaving now.

"And don't talk to me about immigration," Scarz went on, "the country's groaning under the weight of all the bloody people, our national identity has been totally swamped. You don't hear anyone speaking English on the streets round here these days and God knows how many terrorists have strolled in with the so-called refugees. The country just can't cope and the government's doing fuck all, as usual."

"Yes, but immigration's not all down to the EU, is it? Surely you don't believe we can suddenly put up barriers and introduce Australian-type rules at the same time as trying to negotiate trade agreements with people who will find that completely unacceptable?" He stared at Scarz, frustrated. "Anyway, excuse me. I gotta pee." And with that Doug disappeared through the thinning crowd.

Someone tapped Scarz on the shoulder and he turned to see a smartly dressed elderly gentleman smiling faintly at him.

"It's Mr Scarlett, isn't it? David Scarlett? And, when Scarz nodded, he pressed a business card into his palm. "Giles Mortimer, Michael's family solicitor. I wonder if you could stop by my office tomorrow, around ten?" Here he lowered his voice, "You're actually a beneficiary of Michael's – a little something in France, n'est-ce pas?" Scarz wasn't sure but Mortimer seemed to wink as he moved away.

Doug returned: "What's up, mate, seen a ghost?"

"Er, not quite," said Scarz.

"Well I've had enough now, anyway, or I *will* start

seeing them. So, look – I'm off to vote now. You want to join me?"

Scarz hesitated, for once.

"Er … no. You go. I might have one more beer and just sit here for a bit."

GIVE AND TAKE

"Try The Lady," suggested Vera. "They have quite interesting places. Winter lets mostly, but that's all you need, right?"

Lee was looking for somewhere to rent within striking distance of Swindon, after his employers moved there from Slough. Out of the frying pan into the fire, some said, but the town was not that bad. He had done with commuting though. Now, he needed somewhere to tide him over till he was ready to buy. And it would put space between him and Emma. Give him time to think.

The place was in Sherston, just across a gravel courtyard from the crumbling, Cotswold pile where Lady Edith Foxwell lived. Ageing debutante, divorcée and doyenne of the club scene, Edith was a party girl, through and through. She owned a slice of The Embassy Club in Mayfair and counted Marvin Gaye and Roddy Llewellyn amongst her closest friends. But none of that was Lee's scene. The chip on his shoulder was even bigger then; he regarded the privileged at play with scorn.

Her 'cottage' was part stone, with mullioned windows, and part converted stable. The bedroom and bathroom in the stone part felt cosy and secure. But the combined lounge and kitchen in the converted part was more for summer living: scrubbed pine, faded rugs, flagstone floors. The television was basic, the furniture scarred. Someone had spread tin foil on top of the cooker so he wouldn't make a mess of it.

As a place to crash after a day at the office, it was fine. But the weekends were a killer. He tried long, lonely walks to the arboretum. Some Saturday nights he spent in the city, seeking out beer and music, hoping for sex. He ventured out to the village's pubs. But one was a hunting inn, full of braying toffs, the other a rough, beery place, packed with agricultural labourers. A fish out of water in both, he soon retreated.

By Christmas Eve, Lee was desperate. The long break stretched ahead like a nightmare. He drank an unhappy pint in each pub and then demolished some wine at home. There was the usual Christmas rubbish on television. And the mice were taking over. Their droppings were everywhere. He heard their tiny claws scratching on the tin foil. They were running right under the cooker rings. Out of control. He poured a large whisky and set up his stack of cannonballs. By midnight, he was pie-eyed, tearful and hurling oranges at the gimlet-eyed, scampering creatures. He knew they were laughing at him.

The next morning, Lee called his mother. She was delighted; he was coming home for Christmas, after all.

Late December, he made the final break with Emma and put the house on the market. He used the company move as a watershed for their relationship. She was a lovely girl but he'd known it wasn't working after two years. Now, after eight, he felt sour and ashamed. She deserved better and would find it.

Back in Wiltshire, mid-January, someone knocked on the front door, early evening. He supposed it was Edith again, come to explain the measures her gamekeeper was taking to deal with the mice. No-one else ever called, after all. But there, in the glow of the coachlight, warm eyes were glittering beneath a dark fringe. It was Josie, from the office.

"Hello Lee," she said in her low voice. "I thought I'd bring us some supper. Would that be okay?"

"Okay?" he said, "Bloody marvellous, more like. Come on in, girl."

Josie was an attractive and cultured woman who seemed easier in male company. She was almost one of the lads, though essentially a country woman with county style. She'd look good at a horse show, picking over antiques in Stow or having tea in the gardens at Bibury Court. She'd be a whizz at making soups and jellies, training dogs. Everyone seemed to like her, and she was good at her job, too. But a mischievous twinkle was ever present in those dark eyes.

At first, he wondered if she were lesbian. There was something solid and capable about her which he wasn't used to finding in the fragile, suburban women he'd encountered. And then there was that low, husky voice …

As he went to pour her a second glass of red, she hesitated.

"Better not," she said, "I have to drive back, unless …"

"You're not going anywhere," he said, pouring. "It's Saturday tomorrow and I have a perfectly good sofa, if you'd prefer that."

"Prefer that to what?" she said, as they kissed for the first time. He tasted face cream and lipstick and tobacco, discovered a wounded softness there, a need. And a real femininity. Not a trace of girliness, just a soft, real woman. And a woman who wanted him.

With Josie, Sherston was a prison no more. It became a base for exploring. She showed him Bath and the Cotswolds. They went to theatres and movies, ate dinners with friends, took long walks in the country. They smoked, drank wine and talked long into the night about company politics, music and movies, books and writing.

She took to making the teas at Lee's cricket matches and even mastered the scoring, much to the delight of the rest of the team, who'd never had it so good. These were months of easy warmth, laughter and discovery.

Lee felt she was, deep-down, his best friend and always would be. The fact that they were also lovers was incidental to him. And, when he fell for someone else later that year, it never occurred to him that it would break poor Josie's heart.

Years later, he heard that she'd found someone else to love. Richard. They were happy together for many, many years, seemingly partners for life, but then, out of a calm, blue sky, a sudden, blinding light appeared. Richard was transformed, hypnotised. He left Josie for a born-again Christian and a life with her and God. Josie went into deep hiding then, in her little, stone cottage in her Cotswold village.

She reads books now, makes jams and cakes for others. People speak warmly of her but with a faraway look in their eyes. She is seldom seen. Lee often thinks of calling her but he knows she needs to be safe now. Safe from people like him.

THE MESSAGE

It's late autumn and the remaining, yellow leaves drip silver beads in the chill gloom as I pass through the cemetery. The alabaster hound still waits faithfully for his decapitated, young mistress. The one-armed angel gazes sadly over the weeds at the soulless, dog's breakfast of a town. I skirt the puddles and make my way down the hill, past terraced houses slapped up in the railway boom and now rented by absentee landlords to multiple occupants. The houses are forgotten, forlorn and tatty. Their small, front gardens are weed-strewn or concreted over, housing monstrous wheelie-bins, and cars are everywhere, littering the Victorian streets. But, ever the naïve optimist, I am feeling that familiar shred of hope. Like a salmon leaping up a river of dread.

At the door, my brother is haggard and emaciated but mercifully sober, at least for now. I notice that he has managed a shave and I am touched. He attempts his battling-through, cracked grin; the camaraderie of some shared suffering. Like when we were kids. Perhaps he is the oil-smeared group captain, back from a hellish raid on The Ruhr, or the explorer with icy eyebrows, looking up from burying comrades in the frozen Antarctic. But the grin doesn't work anymore. Not really. It comes out as the leer of a grubby old man. But I understand and that's all that matters to him. And I can feel the beat of real warmth behind it.

He moves the unpaid bills and the years-old magazines and has me sit on the sofa in his small, cluttered house, hemmed in by his few possessions. A small regiment of empty wine bottles stands to attention around me, waiting. I know he won't let me touch them. Not yet. Wooden boxes like small coffins hold his cherished, old singles. Cardboard cartons of unsent greeting cards from his untended business cover most of the remaining space on the carpet. It is an arrangement that makes him feel secure and me scream inside with claustrophobia.

He has rewound the Victorian clock on the mantel-piece, but he hasn't corrected the time. I hear it steadily ticking down our lives. Both ashtrays are overflowing and ash mixes with thick dust on the glass table top. He carefully hands me a mug of coffee. It's way too strong but he presents it with such pride that I accept it gracefully.

He rolls a skinny cigarette with wavering, yellow fingers and lights it.

"Old Holborn," he says with a wink. But rather than savouring the aroma, I just feel my eyes sting from the smoke. He plays me music from the sixties: *There's A Place, This Boy, Yes It Is, Autumn Almanac*. Songs we sang together in harsh and perfect harmony, years ago, up in front of the adoring crowds. I see the guitar gathering dust in the corner, but I say nothing.

He joins me on the sofa and leafs through old photos. The tears start, as I knew they would, when he gets to

Jill, the pretty girl he should have married thirty years ago. And the only one of his women I ever cared for. I am hoping he doesn't feel me shrink from the maudlin mood I see developing – and the threat that lurks therein.

Then, sensing that I might leave, he stumbles out to fetch his latest, near-completed painting. The schooner Result is ploughing her way through a rampant North Sea. He describes the challenge of capturing the colour and movement of the sea, the crest on the bow, the heaviness of the swell. He talks about his research into the ship, of the need to get the arrangement of the sails consistent with historical detail and presumed wind direction, to say nothing of perspective. And every piece of rigging must be authentic, or he will be lambasted by some pernickety, old skipper. Because credibility is everything.

I say: "It's wonderful, mate. Fantastically accurate, but also, so full of light and life."

And I mean it. He sees that and grasps my arm gratefully.

"I can still do it, then?"

"Of course, you can. It's in your blood. And in your heart. Look at what you've already done, for God's sake; you should have more confidence."

He smiles ruefully at me like that was asking for the world.

I feel safe, relaxed, almost blasé in his company, as if half-drunk myself. At some point, I lie down and start to drift off. I'm with the friends in the photos. They are laughing together as the music plays. I see that my brother is making them laugh and Jill is by his side, squeezing his arm indulgently. I'm falling down, down into the comforting, cotton-wool, safety-net of the past when a massive bolt of electricity shoots and shudders through me like a heart attack.

I know right away that I have to save him. Save him from himself. There's just too much to lose. And it's deadly urgent. But I'm underwater now. I'm groping for the light, stretching to break the surface.

And then I'm awake. And I remember. I'm more than five years too late.

*

The next morning, I'm still thinking about it. Was it a message from my dead brother? Or, perhaps more likely, from my inner self, my subconscious? Is it really myself I have to save? While there's still just a little time.

At breakfast, I am looking again at the painting on the wall. I see the astonishing skill, the authentic detail, the hard-won colour and movement of the sea. But, most of all, I see the courage of the artist. And I understand.

I understand the message.

HUMAN NATURE

He became aware of it soon after entering the kitchen. Some slight movement, some minute refraction of the light must have caught the corner of his eye. He heard no buzzing or fluttering, but he could see it on the inside of the window by the courtyard door. He watched it crawl laboriously up the UPVC surround onto the pane, tiny wings trembling, only to slip from the glass and tumble to the work surface, where it lay on its back, momentarily stunned by the shock or, perhaps, pausing for breath. Soon after, a horrible wriggling ensued; a desperate struggle to right itself. Finally, it must have gritted its tiny teeth before embarking on the unvarying ascent once more, with an identical outcome.

Frank observed this several times. He found himself admiring the dogged determination of the tiny creature, though puzzled at its inability to learn from experience.

It must be dying, he thought, *or it's starved of light or air, or something's happened to it. Maybe it's wounded. Maybe it's out of its tiny mind, if it ever had one.*

He studied the insect. It wasn't a housefly. It looked more like a flying ant. But its jointed, black body was longer, thinner than that. And more mobile. He admired the detail of its tiny form. Such complexity, even in the smallest things. Was that just evolution or was something else at work here?

Frank had not found God, but then he never went look-ing. He kept himself to himself. Walked with a soft tread. Saw the machinations of religion as patronising, self-serv-ing and sometimes dangerous. At the same time, he found it hard to accept that the whole, immaculate world of na-ture had just developed itself. From what – a hot soup of neutrons, electrons and protons? And why was it so beau-tiful, so perfect? How come it all interlocked, like some trillion-piece jigsaw? Why were so many of its structures tied to Fibonacci number sequences? Why was there such a perfect, delicate balance, such interdependency? Was he supposed to believe that was all just natural selection? The survival of the fittest? Over almost fourteen billion years, admittedly. But was that it? Really? Or were God and Nature somehow the same thing?

It was all happening now, he saw. Thorax writhing, abdomen curling, wings fluttering nervously. It didn't seem to be damaged in any physical way. But he didn't like the desperation in that writhing. Surely, this was not purely instinctive behaviour. There was fear there. Neediness. Primal fear and panic. It was going to de-stroy itself.

He tore a sheet of kitchen roll from the holder and tucked it under the quivering body, lifting it gently back onto the glass, providing support; a fallback position, a safety net. But it didn't seem to recognise its new sav-iour. It scuttled across the paper and dropped to the work surface. He tried again. And then again.

Jude had come in and was watching him.

"You're not doing it right," she said. "Here, let me."

"You're not going to hurt him, are you?"

"No, I won't hurt it."

He passed her the paper and watched as she did the same thing, with the same result.

"Try to get him on the paper," he suggested.

"What the *fuck* do you think I'm trying to do?"

"I mean *keep* him on the paper. Then we can take him outside."

"How is that going to help it?" she asked, but she tried anyway. The insect ran off the paper again.

Angela came to join them.

"What's going on?" she asked, in an authoritative tone.

"Nothing. Just a rescue mission," said Jude.

She peered over.

"Ugh! It's a fly. Just kill it."

"It's not a fly," said Frank, aware of the defensive tone in his voice. "It's a beetle or something." He didn't know what the hell it was, but he thought a beetle might elicit more sympathy, somehow; support his weakening cause.

Angela ignored him.

"Flies crawl on shit all day. You do *not* want them in our kitchen, spreading disease."

"It's not a fly," he repeated.

"Oh, *bugger* it. He's off again," said Jude.

"Let me see," said Angela.

Jude scooped the insect onto the paper again and passed it quickly to Angela who immediately scrunched the paper into a tight ball.

"Problem solved," she said, with a twisted grin, raising her fist in triumph.

"You've killed him," said Frank. "You had no right to do that."

"It was a little underhand," said Jude.

"Whatever," said Angela. "There are more important things in life."

"*He* was alive. *He* had a life."

"It was a fly. A disgusting, shit-eating fly. You twat."

"It was probably dying anyway," said Jude.

"You had no right," repeated Frank, more softly.

Angela looked at him with scorn.

"You're so soft, Frank. Soft as shit."

HANGING WITH THE BOSS

I have never cared for public loos and avoid them when I can. Of course, no-one likes a toilet that stinks, or is wet, or just plain disgusting and, let's face it, there are plenty of those around. I know that. We all know that. But that's not the issue here. I'm talking about decency and modesty, about trying to be a human being rather than a beast.

So, tell me. How come you ladies always get a private cubicle while we blokes are expected to stand in a row with complete strangers and dangle it over a bloody trough without even a modesty panel between us, more often than not?

It doesn't help that, since puberty, I have always had nagging doubts about my 'bits,' as my missus delights in calling them. I think most men have, though we pretend otherwise. Well, you have to, don't you? Pretend, I mean. Breezy confidence is essential, or others will assume from any natural shyness or reticence that there is some dire inadequacy you have to cover up. Or so we imagine, in our tortured minds …

I'd bet even the urinal designer wouldn't dare suggest modesty panels for fear his boss would say something like:

"Why would you want the extra cost of those, lad – a little something to hide, have you?"

And so, the macho culture prevails, condemning us all to endless indignity.

I should add that many women have reassured me personally about my *John Thomas* and I believe them. Really, I do. And, God knows, I've seen enough of the things in my life to know that mine's there or thereabouts, even compared to those show-offs on the naturist beaches or the foolhardy lads on that very strange dating show on Channel Four. But still, that teenage angst never completely goes away. Happily, I know I'm not alone in this because, over the years, I have observed four coping strategies used by fellow-sufferers:

The most common is the *straight-ahead guy*. He always faces the front, like he's not really there. He feigns absorption in the adverts for *Crimestoppers* or *The Samaritans* or ribbed and colourful condoms, but is careful to avoid those for erectile dysfunction, lest we think he suffers. He will follow closely the antics of a spider crawling across the wall. If there are graffiti, he will study them minutely as if they were Banksy's latest works of art. He will never look in your direction and only looks down when needs must.

Then there are the *self-admirers*. They never take their eyes off their own member. It's as if they are in love with it. Seeking solace in it. Or deeply concerned about it. Or perhaps they are just being hugely careful to make sure all the pee goes in the right direction. Maybe theirs has a wayward tendency. Or perhaps *they* do. These guys are no trouble, but they are kind of creepy.

The *comparers* are more brazen. They want to know what yours looks like, simple as that. They may even initiate a conversation. Some favourite remarks include: "This is where the nobs hang out, then" (basic but undeniable) or (in a pub): "We don't *buy* beer, do we? We rent the bloody stuff." This one is sometimes followed by a mordant: "It's all piss, anyway."

Whatever they say, you feel obliged to glance across as you sense them grinning at you like an idiot. You might exchange some nonsense with them but, at the end of the conversation comes the coup de grâce, when their eyes drop for a sneak-peek before they turn away. As if they had to sign off to both parties: you and your silent friend. Like it was a dog to pat. I can only assume that these guys are cursed with even more angst than me.

Quite a few men fall into the final group: the *hiders*. They have abandoned the contest. Given up. They shun the trough completely and make a beeline for the cubicles. Now, much as I sympathise with their need for modesty and humanity, the cubicles are for more serious business! Many times, I see guys desperate for a poo but unable to get into a cubicle because the bloke inside is clearly standing and peeing into the bowl, probably without even lifting the seat. You can hear it. You'd think they'd have the decency to at least *pretend* they were doing number twos …

Anyway, all this gives you a clear idea that I have been hyper-conscious of the goings-on in toilets all my life. I put myself in the *straight-ahead* group. I might prefer to be a *hider* but I don't think that's right, somehow. If you're afraid of heights, go climb a mountain. We all need to face up to our issues in life, don't we?

71

In the offices where I work, toilets are usually cleaner and smarter. There might be single-use, cotton towels with smart baskets to drop them in. There might be scented soaps in dispensers and powerful air-driers into which you insert your hands, trustingly. Music might be playing softly. And yet, even in this rarefied environment, modesty panels are typically absent. It seems very strange to me that we come out of meetings in our smart suits with our perfectly knotted ties, meetings where we have been so careful to mind our p's and q's and talked in such nuanced and respectful tones, only to whip this hairy, deeply animal thing out of our trousers in front of each other. I really don't want to know these guys that well!

It may be a sparkling, white urinal with automatic, antiseptic washing but the issues remain the same for me. As a *straight-ahead guy*, it's *more* problematic, if anything, because there's nothing to look at. Zippo. No adverts, no graffiti, no insect life that could survive. I can only inspect the tile grout, check the water pipe for rust, try to make out a reflection of myself.

I am doing this one day when Gene, the newish American President and CEO, walks in.

"Hi Mark. How ya doing, buddy?"

I glance in his direction as I must. His face radiates enthusiasm and drive. He is looking at my face. He doesn't seem to have noticed that I am urinating. I say, "Hi, Gene," and quickly resume *straight-ahead guy* mode, trying to control a schoolboy titter at the sound of what I just said. Hygiene. In this antiseptic place. Funny. The only thing to observe on the pristine, white-tiled wall is my reflected smirk. But then, out of the corner of my eye, I see that he is undressing. I am alarmed and can't bear to look but, in the tiles, I can just make out that he has folded his trousers right back, out of the way, and seems to be removing a further layer – is it a vest or something? This goes on for some time. In all my years of toilet voyeurism, I have never known anything like this. Finally, he lets out a sigh and starts to pee. We are both relieved. I am finishing up when I sense him looking over again.

"So, how's the new job, Mark? Exciting?"

I glance back and he is looking straight at my face with that gleaming intensity of his. I do up my fly and move over to the basin.

"It's okay. I'm enjoying it, Gene, but I'm not sure I'd use the word *exciting*."

"You wouldn't?" He appears to be reassembling him-self, robotically. Fleetingly, I wonder if he is really an android.

"I'm not sure the world of business is ever *exciting*, is it?"

He comes over and starts washing his hands.

"So, what *do* you find exciting?"

"More creative stuff, I suppose. Music, art, writing maybe?"

He's piercing me now with those rigorous, blue eyes, calculating, reappraising. I'm cursing myself for being drawn into a career-limiting remark. How could I have been so stupid? I think his bizarre toilet behaviour must have thrown me.

"Those are wonderful things, Mark, I know. They excite me, as well. But you are *so* wrong about business. It's fascinating, wholly absorbing and yes – exciting too. Working with bright people, developing strategies, executing plans, the wealth of possibilities … the possibility of wealth …"

He is glinting with latent excitement. I'm wondering if he just thought of that natty little juxtaposition. His hand is gripping my shoulder now and he has moved his face closer to mine. I am getting a whiff of his seriously expensive after-shave.

"Don't hold back, Mark. Get involved. *Immerse* yourself. You're gonna find out what I mean. And you're gonna love it. I know this, believe me."

He slaps me on the shoulder, grins aggressively, then takes a peeled, raw onion from a paper bag and starts to eat it like an apple.

"Hangover cure," he says, seeing the horror on my face. "It's the only thing that works. You should try it."

As we left that toilet, I understood. It was a wake-up call, a warning shot. Not about the onion, but about my career. I didn't really have one before, to be honest, but then, right from that moment, I did. I worked hard; *immersed* myself, I suppose. And the more I did, the less like work it became. I actually wanted to be there. And he was right. In the end, it was exciting. I got to see toilets all over the world. Expensive ones.

A colleague reminded me, a few days after that incident. Soon after landing the job, Gene was commuting eighty miles and working crazy hours. One misty morning he must still have been asleep when his Daimler piled into a milk float and he put himself in hospital for several weeks. Milk floats don't sound solid, do they? But they are. Very. Ask the Daimler. Or Gene. Happily, the milkman was watching from someone's doorstep at the time. Aghast, I should imagine. Anyway, that day in the toilet was months later and I had forgotten all about the crash. But Gene was still wearing all manner of surgical supports and dressings, apparently. Quite unabashed.

What it is to have confidence. Or just to keep the confidence we are born with.

SOLACE

Every Saturday, he buys the pink newspaper. They sit in companionable silence for much of the morning. Every so often, they trade snippets. From his newspaper; from her laptop.

"You can pick up Carnival shares for under ten pounds, now," he says, "down seventy-three percent in the last three months. Could be a good bet, long-term."

"The cruise people? Whatever. My cash is stuck in the company, right now."

"You can dividend it out. Or the company could invest."

His items risk boring or irritating her. He knows that. Sometimes it's economic or financial stuff that she doesn't want to understand, but he persists. If it surprises or excites him, then it must interest her, surely? Anyway, she needs to know.

"Good Lord, I can't believe it. Anne's getting married again," she says.

"Your friend from Palmerston North?"

"No, that's Alice, for God's sake! Anne, from Christchurch. Alice is married to Stu. You *know* that."

She relates things discovered in emails and social media postings or from trawling the Internet. It's often stuff from her home country on the other side of the world.

Or concerning people he only vaguely remembers. She seems to want him to care about them, still.

But he finds her stories irrelevant now, and long-winded, and his eyes glaze over. When she sees that, she hates him for it. He is irritated because he wants to read on Saturday mornings, not listen. Eventually they snap at each other and silence is resumed, apart from the tapping of keys, the rustle of the paper and someone singing, far away …

In due course, one of them says, "Shall we make lunch and do the crosswords?" Briefly, the perfunctory question of what to have for lunch is raised, but they already know the answer.

The kitchen can be a dangerous place for them. Generally, she has firm views, but he is more pliable. But he's not pliable in the kitchen. Not at all. He knows the right way to do things and can't tolerate people getting it needlessly wrong. Not listening. Messing up. Spoiling things.

Miraculously, though, there is one thing they agree on. Precisely. Entirely. Even in the kitchen. After years perfecting it. And that is how to make the Saturday sandwich.

It starts with the grill, warming it up, plates below. He defrosts the four slices of hand-cut, multi-grain bread in the microwave for exactly twenty seconds and then spreads two of the slices with butter, adding a little Hellman's mayonnaise to hers, a little Heinz tomato ketchup to his.

Only she can test the avocados for ripeness. He sees her pressing them to her nose, then squeezing the ends gently. The first one that passes the test is halved, slippery egg-stone prised out, green flesh scooped, then lathered on the other two slices of bread.

While she uses scissors to cut four or five bacon rashers in half and assembles them on the grill, he washes and chops mushrooms for a pan already bubbling with olive oil, butter and cracked, black pepper. She prefers the mushrooms peeled but he won't do that, despite her resentment. Pointless. While she watches over the bacon and mushrooms as they cook, he chops fresh tomatoes, then pours fruit juice into glasses, lightening with tonic water.

By now, the bacon hisses and spits as it grills. The clogged, extractor fan isn't coping. He flings open a window and sees blue fumes curl away like smoke above her shoulder. As the bacon crisps, it's time to assemble. She lays the tomato pieces on the avocado spread and grinds black pepper over them. He tumbles the sizzling bacon pieces in kitchen towel, briefly, then places them on the tomatoes and covers with the buttery mushrooms, straight from the pan. Finally, she adorns them with a crown of freshly torn rocket leaves. The other bread slices are pressed firmly on top and the plates retrieved from the warmer. Then he cuts the sandwiches with the big knife, four quarters for her, two halves for him, and places them on the warmed plates on trays, each with its drink and a clean napkin by the side.

They return to the living room with their prizes. This is the only time they sit side by side on the sofa. He finds the crossword section and folds the paper with precision.

"Hamilton and Mudd," he announces, referring to this week's setters.

Their legs almost touch as they bite into their sandwiches.

"Yum," she says, and picks up a pen.

*

When they finish, she says: "I'll miss our little rituals."

He is staring out of the window and mumbles: "Me too."

He knows he'll still buy the paper, still cheat on the Polymath, still finish the cryptic crossword, eventually. Maybe he'll still make a bacon sandwich, though the ripeness of the avocado will be a guess. And he's not sure it will taste as good, somehow. Any of it.

*

Later, he steps outside and sits on the bench with the paper, but he doesn't read it. He is looking at the garden they made together. Clusters of bluebells are bobbing in front of the purple clematis. Hanging baskets are festooned with white, pink and lilac petunias. The evening air is heavy with honeysuckle and jasmine. Somewhere a wren is singing, then a blackbird. He sees a perfect spider's web spun between two roses. In the distance, a train whistles faintly as a ladybird settles on his hand and crawls recklessly into his palm.

He finds himself pondering the same question he has asked himself so many times: *How do you know when you really love someone?*

Is it when you *want* them all the time? Lust after them. When you're obsessed with the smell of their body, their hair, the way they look at you and smile. And turned on by the way they move, the desire that glows behind their eyes. Or is that just chemicals? A passion headed for a car wreck. Another burned-out chassis on life's hard shoulder.

Is it when you want to *be with* someone all the time and something is missing whenever they are not there? And you feel lost and pointless in their absence. An empty shell. A void with one sad bastard sitting in it. Or is that just neediness, some pathetic dependence?

Or is it when you get that quiet, comfortable feeling from truly knowing another human being? Hours without speaking, yet totally at ease. Finding solace. Sharing the familiar. Looking to give each other little parcels of thoughtfulness. Loved routines that make us feel so damned good, deep inside. Or is that just settling for less? Complacency.

Or is the sad truth that it can be any or all of those, but you will never know until it's over. Until she walks away …

THE HEADMASTER'S STUDY

October 1967 and Friday the twentieth is just another school day. He takes the diesel railcar to Moor Park as usual, shuffles through The Spinney and enters the tall, iron gates with the school's crest. He's in the fourth year now and he is fourteen years old.

It was not far to come from Northwood Hills and the flat they've been living in for ten months. It is always a flat to him, never an 'apartment'. Number twenty forms part of a 1940s block called Northcote. The gravel drive from the main road is pitted. Brown puddles in the potholes can drench your whole foot if you aren't looking or splash you all over if a tyre from a passing car slops into one. The dingy, cream walls are scuffed and patchy, the metal window-frames painted that lurid, dark green found on council estates. The stairs smell of cats' piss and simmering sprouts as you make your way up. The flat itself is not too bad after Mum has organised everything and put on her brave face. In his room, he tacks his 'Garden of Earthly Delights' Bosch print and his 'Victorian Moustaches' poster to the wall and plays 'Waterloo Sunset'. After that, everything is pretty much okay.

The family rupture has been a long time coming. Dad is unstable. That much is obvious, even to Rob.

Mum and Phil bear the brunt of it: scathing verbal abuse screamed at them most days. He sees it wound them; diminish them. Like thrown acid, eating through the flesh of their self-confidence. And, occasionally, there is physical violence or, at least, the imminent threat of it. But, on other days, Dad can be charming, amusing in a quirky way, almost considerate. He is manic depressive or bi-polar or something. They never really know. Alcohol almost certainly fuels his rages. Mum is getting more frightened of Dad, even as she quietly works to build her escape fund. But the carving knife under his pillow is the last straw. By late 1966, she is desperate to leave.

Rob sees all this coming, of course, but he is not sure where he stands. Dad has been okay with him. Phil can never do anything right but Rob has always been Dad's blue-eyed boy for some reason; his fledgling, his protégé, the child he invests in, the son that makes him shine with pride and from whom he asks and expects great things. Dad tells him this often.

But it goes beyond even that. Rob feels the weight of all Dad's love and hope. It feels dangerously heaped on him, balanced precariously on his head, bearing down on his narrow, schoolboy shoulders. And to disappoint Dad would be to inflict a deep, personal wound. More than that, it could take away his very future. Rob knows that, so maybe he will flee before that happens. Because he knows, in the end, that he can only let him down.

"I need you to make a big decision, Rob," Mum says one day. "Do you want to come with me and Phil or stay with your Dad?" She is careful to make it clear: He should take his time, give it serious thought. She will not try to persuade him, either way.

It is a reasonable question and he understands why she has to ask it. He can stay with Dad and it will be okay. He will be safe and loved, given everything Dad can give.

But it is also a scary question. If he stays, he will see much less of Phil and Mum, and he is very close to them. In the worst times, it has become the three of them versus Dad. But then he always feels guilty about that afterwards. And, if *he* goes too, Dad will be alone.

*

The long drive, lined with horse-chestnuts, stretches away past the cricket pavilion and the great spread of rugby pitches. The water meadows beyond are lush and the lake sparkles in the watery, autumn sunshine. The 1930s clock tower reaches up like the squat neck of some mythical beast above the distant square of school buildings, reddish-brown stone against playing-field green. Scatterings of boys in rumpled, grey suits and loosened ties straggle along the drive, shuffling through leaves, pausing to search for husks. Occasionally a satchel fight erupts or a hail of conkers is launched at some unwitting target.

In the classroom, they dump satchels on desks, swap notes on homework, exchange abuse and fight for space on the radiator. In the assembly hall, they whisper and fidget through the sermon, roar through *Hills of the North, Rejoice!* mumble prayers and then stream out to *Bach's*

Toccata and Fugue in D Minor. Lifted above the cynicism they wear on their sleeves, the collective energy is palpable. They are the young, the inspired. The chosen ones.

Halfway through the second period he is called out of class.

He feels the blood rise hot in his cheeks as his name is called. Singled out – for what? The chaplain, a kindly but formal man, says simply:

"The Headmaster wants to speak to you, Irwin. Come with me."

Has he been spotted smoking in the water meadows? Or that day they sneaked up to the top of the clock tower? Or is it something else?

The chaplain's brisk pace and withdrawn manner brook no discussion. Then Rob realises that they aren't going to the Headmaster's room at all but to his private house. This is unprecedented. He has never heard of a boy being taken there.

PJ himself is at the door, looking oddly vulnerable and smiling faintly, hand restraining the wayward blond curls prematurely thinning above his high forehead. Maybe it's not trouble, after all.

"Thank you, John. Come in, Irwin. We'll just go on up to my study."

Rob notices that the harsh edge is absent from PJ's voice. He wonders if it is just a device he uses to find volume for class or assembly.

"Sit down, Irwin."

He sits on the chair in front of an elegant desk. He expects PJ to sit on the other side, but instead he perches on the corner, arranges his gown and turns his blue eyes on Rob's.

"I'm sorry to drag you from your class, but I have some very bad news for you, Irwin. I'm afraid it's going to be a shock."

An incongruous thrill of electricity shorts its way through him but then he shivers slightly.

"It's your father."

He is looking at Rob intensely now, searching his eyes. Rob feels at his mercy.

"I'm very sorry to tell you that your father has died, Irwin."

A lurch inside. Moments of terrible silence. And then questions rushing in from all sides.

"But how, sir? Are you sure? I was with him just a few weeks ago. We were in Cornwall. He wasn't ill."

A pause. PJ is looking at him sorrowfully. He speaks gently.

"It seems he took his own life. I'm so sorry."

Rob searches frantically for ways in which that phrase could be misinterpreted and, desolate, finds none.

"You mean he killed himself, sir."

"That's what the police are saying, yes."

"The police? But he can't have. Why? How?"

"We probably shouldn't dwell …"

"How, sir?"

"Gas. He used the gas oven at home. And they found empty bottles: whisky, barbiturates."

The finality of it starts to sink in. This was no mistake, no cry for help. He set out to die. And now Rob sees him, stretched out on the cold kitchen floor in that suburban house, amongst the detritus of his death kit. His Dad. His dear old, desperate Dad. He had no idea how desperate. His Dad who he will never see again because he is dead now and always will be. For ever and ever. Amen.

He is silent then, for quite a while. PJ is saying that Rob's brother has been contacted at Hornsey Art College. They are still trying to reach his mother at her school. Is it Townfield in Hayes? Is that right? Anyway, it would be best if he stayed here until the rest of the family are home at the flat in Northwood Hills.

"I'll leave you now, Irwin. Give you some time to gather your thoughts. Mrs Price-Jones will pop in a bit later on."

"Wait sir, please. Do you know who found him?" he asks.

PJ consults his papers.

"A neighbour from number sixty-two. Joyce?"

Rob nods, lips pursed.

"Your father asked if he might borrow some shears. It was arranged that Joyce would drop them round this morning."

So, he had even selected the person to find his body, he realises. And his heart aches for poor Joyce, who never deserved that. He supposes Dad was making sure it was not one of them. And again, he is struck by the deadly plan. A rational man, planning sanely, methodically, for the ultimate insanity.

PJ leaves him then, alone in his study, and Rob is thinking that he spoke in a very kindly way, but how odd it is that he never once used his first name, or reached out to comfort him with a hug, a firm grasp of the shoulder or even just a manly handshake. Perhaps the absence of Rob's tears confused him. Or perhaps nothing could ever justify such a lapse of protocol in PJ's tight, little world.

Rob goes to the window and gazes out at the trees. Silver birches are shedding leaves of a musty-coloured yellow. The Kinks' new song *Autumn Almanac* has started, somewhere in his head, on some endless loop. Gradually, questions begin to form like dark monsters, looming above him; questions that will never be resolved and will never ever go away.

"Why?" "Why, Dad?"

And, a little later, "Was it my fault, Dad?"

Even then, he knows. He is no longer the boy who entered that room. He has aged ten years, perhaps more. He will be a boy apart now.

The clock ticks. The rain eases. The leaves drip. And still no-one comes. He stares out at the trees with the song still in his head but sees only Dad. Dad at The Dog and Duck raising a beer to a buxom barmaid with dark, wavy hair and almond-shaped eyes. Like his phone pad doodles. Dad at Warnham Pond, staring dreamily at the mill. Dad singing *I'm Happy on the Prairie All the Day* in the car as they escape to the country and then *Farmer Gray* at each rural county border. Dad playing Charles Penrose's *Laughing Policeman* and making them laugh until tears run down all their faces, even Mum's.

Dad with his Plain Jane toffees and his Pascal's fruit bon-bons and his Three Nuns tobacco. Dad with his chest stripped bare at the first, faint sun of spring or wearing his dun-coloured, short-sleeved shirts or his smart, Hector Powe suits with the skinny-knotted ties and the brogues. Dad puffing his pipe behind the Guardian and pretending that he isn't watching television like the rest of them. Charming, handsome Dad. Dad when they are in Ljubljana, mimicking the waiter, Charlie Chaplin's double, and they all sing the *Dardanelles* song.

Dad bribing him. A ten-shilling note for each book read: *Treasure Island, David Copperfield, Lord of the Flies*. Dad and the school report, zeroing in on the only subject where Rob hasn't come top of the class. Does Rob misunderstand the sarcasm? Is it a gentle tease, in fact? Or is Dad honestly, seriously alarmed at Rob's lowly, second place in Religious Instruction?

Then, all those times of Dad not being there. Putting Rob's new train set on top of the wardrobe with all the other still-wrapped presents and then disappearing for Christmas. Or leaving Phil and Rob to play on Cornish beaches for hours on end, alone. Or vanishing from the family home for days, shutting off the power lest they be wasteful. Or warm. And then, finally, the dread sound of that stiff, garden brush – eerie first signal of his return – rhythmically sweeping all the leaves from the path and all the simple joys from their hearts.

Dad making Mum cry. Dad frothing at the mouth in fury.

Dad crying and calling him Ducky.

Dad so desperate to be loved while he drove them all away.

THE BAND

Kieran always had a sense of rhythm; a feel for the beat. When Mersey Sound exploded onto the music scene, he was just ten years old, but he was already dancing to the radio or singing harmonies with his brother. Martin was older. His schoolboy acne had started to fade, and he was good-looking now. He had a proper, semi-acoustic guitar and a Beatle-haircut.

Kieran was always tapping away on his thighs or on kitchen work surfaces or raiding the sewing-box for knitting needles with which to hit carefully positioned biscuit tins and his mother's cherished, brass sweet-trays. He experimented by part-filling the tins or covering them with cloth to change the sounds they made. He put plasticine in one of the sweet trays to get cymbals with contrasting tones.

Those days, even when he was just sitting, one of his knees would be jigging up and down endlessly.

"Ants in your pants?" they'd say with a smirk but, in truth, he was irritating the shit out of everyone.

His mother quietly binned the dented sweet trays and bought him a rubber practice pad and a pair of real drumsticks for his fourteenth birthday. That was it. Within six months, he had saved up for his first kit. It was a cheap, Olympic set-up in blue sparkle, but it sounded okay. Even then, he knew that the ideal was a Rogers bass drum, a Ludwig snare, tom-toms by Premier and Zyn or Super-Zyn cymbals. But that was in his dreams. For now, he just wanted to start playing.

When he first set up in the living-room, he couldn't believe how deafening it was. No-one could remain in the room. It was a detached house, but the neighbours were soon bitching. In response, Kieran bought soft brushes and limited daytime practice hours were negotiated, backed up by the practice pad. He quickly learned to co-ordinate the bass drum and hi-hat pedals. Then he focused on the snare. He experimented with all the different sounds: snare on; snare off; rim shots; cross sticking. Pretty soon, he could do single rolls and triplets and got the hang of segueing from snare to the three tom-toms and back again.

He took a few lessons, too. Albert was a sinewy guy in his thirties who was into jazz. He held the left-hand drumstick in the classical way and taught Kieran the "ten-to-two" cymbal sequence, how to read music for drums, how to do double-rolls and paradiddles and how to use the brushes effectively.

By now, Martin was pretty good on the guitar and had started writing some really good songs. He was looking to form a band.

"Albert reckons you're not bad," he said one day. "I've got a couple of guys lined-up for lead and bass now. You could sit in for our first practice, if you like? Just temporary, of course, but we haven't found a drummer yet. You'd be helping us out – if you don't balls it up too much, that is."

Kieran practised like crazy for the next week. Martin told him some of the tracks they were planning to cover, and he played along with the records.

He was nervous as hell before the first session. These guys were musicians and all several years older. But he needn't have worried. From the outset it worked. Kieran was a natural and they were all learning together, anyway. Strings broke, microphones crackled with static or whined with feedback, amplifiers buzzed unexpectedly, harmonies missed badly and ended in laughter. Dave on lead guitar struggled to master his new wah-wah pedal. Kieran dropped a drumstick once or twice and the bass drum tended to slide forward so he needed a right leg like Twizzle to keep playing. Once he knocked the hi-hat over with an almighty crash.

Over the weeks, though, they got better and much tighter. They introduced a few of Martin's songs to their selection of covers from The Kinks, The Beatles and The Yardbirds, along with standards such as Bye-Bye Johnnie and Knock on Wood. Martin was frontman on vocals and rhythm guitar with occasional harmonica or tambourine, but they could all sing quite well. They bought an old J2 van and Martin painted a picture on the front of Kieran's bass drum. They decided to call themselves "The Gates of Dawn."

The first gig was set for March the tenth at The Fisheries Inn and all the gang were there. They opened with "Jumping Jack Flash" and went down a storm.

The Fisheries became a regular spot and they played in a few other pubs and then a big dance at a hotel in

St. Alban's. Kieran loved every minute. At heart he was a shy lad, if a little precocious at times, but behind his drums he grew in confidence. He knew he was pretty good by now. Some even said "child prodigy" about him; he was only just fifteen. Every time at The Fisheries, the crowd would ask for a drum solo and Kieran would be the star for five minutes, often getting the loudest applause of the night. He adored the attention and the drunken adulation, but he also loved just being in a band and playing with these guys: his mates and his brother.

*

One Sunday in August, Kieran woke to the sounds of the band tuning up.

Oh shit, I've forgotten a band practice, he thought in alarm and quickly dressed and went downstairs. In the living-room, a good-looking guy of about twenty-two was lounging behind a Premier kit, smoking and twirling a drumstick. Martin came over and walked Kieran out of the room.

"I'm sorry, I just didn't realise there was a practice today," Kieran started to say.

"No, well I didn't need to tell you because we've found our drummer now. That's Chris Fox in there."

"But I'm the drummer."

"You were always a stand-in, Kieran. I made that clear from the start. And anyway, you just didn't practise enough, did you? You can't be a lazy sod in this game. Sorry, mate."

Martin went back inside.

Face streaming with hot tears of hurt and frustration,

Kieran kicked a hole in his bass drum and broke his sticks. He never played again.

*

Years later, when they were old men, Martin was diagnosed with cancer. It had metastasized. They told him he had just months to live.

"There's something I need to tell you, Kieran," he said one day. "It's difficult for me, but it's the right thing to do. It's only right that you should know."

"Know what?"

"About the band." He paused, and then looked directly into Kieran's eyes. "You were a terrific drummer, really talented; the star of the band, in fact. Everybody said so. I pushed you out because I was jealous as hell. You were hogging the limelight – and I wanted it all to myself."

"You did? Really? Jesus. Fucking hell, Martin … and the practising?"

"You could have done more, but you were better than the rest of us anyway; you had an extraordinary, natural gift. It was a terrible thing to do. I'm so sorry, mate."

Kieran thought back on his life. There had never been anything to replace the drumming. Nothing to bring out his extrovert, exhibitionist side. Nothing which had felt just right because of some inborn talent. Nothing that had brought the kinship of the band. He had conformed to a corporate career with deep reluctance and something akin to dread. It had brought financial security and stress in equal measure but rarely satisfaction and never even the smallest amount of adulation.

"Fucking hell," he said again, quietly, and walked to the window. Leaves were falling from the silver birch and fat drops of rain were lashing the pane, running down like tears.

After all these years, Kieran knew Martin was looking for absolution. After a couple of minutes, he came back and laid his hand heavily on his brother's shoulder.

"You old bastard," he said.

THE LATE SHIFT SPECIALIST

The ageing schnauzer meanders along the pavement, lifts its leg and marks the gate pillar. Then it looks back at the girl. She loves it when he looks at her like that, ears pricked, head tilted; a fluffy, question mark of a dog.

"Go on, Cedric," she says, "yer daft, old bugger."

She flicks the lead and, reassured, he trots on, nose to the ground, snuffling in the grass and weeds that grow from the base of the garden walls.

"You never said you'd bring a dog," says the man.

"What of it?"

"You just never said."

"And you never said: 'no dogs.' Anyway, he's no trouble."

"We'll have to see, won't we?"

They walk on in the gloom, past rows of identical 1930s semis in varying states of disrepair. She sees a rusting Ford Capri on axle stands in one front garden, an old bath and some tyres in another. A net curtain twitches and she glimpses an old lady looking fearful and bewildered. Dark rain clouds are building over the cemetery.

"How far is it?"

"Not far."

"How long will we be? Only, I could tie him, for a little while."

"Forget about the bloody dog."

She looks at him, then. Seedy is the word – pretty much what she expected. Deep pools of eyes that avoid contact, thinning ginger hair; a grubby raincoat of a man.

"I was only saying," she says, quietly.

The first, fat raindrops are hitting the pavement. He looks over at her.

"New to this, then?" he asks.

"Yeah, but I'm up for it. Definitely."

He looks her over.

"How old d'you say you was?"

"Eighteen."

He's nodding and grinning with big eyes like she's shared a joke.

"You'll have danced a bit, though, wiv yer mates and that?"

"'Course I have. Reggae mostly."

"That figures."

"What d'you mean?"

"That you'd like reggae. It makes sense."

"For a black girl, you mean."

"If you like. No need to get uppity about it."

"Don't go stereotyping me. All right?"

He closes his eyes and shakes his head.

"Jesus fucking wept," he says.

They come to a building that was once a church hall. He stops and grabs her arm, she yanks on Cedric's lead and he starts to bark. A middle-aged woman with a child comes past under a scarlet umbrella and throws her a sharp look.

"Is this it, then?" she says.

"It's a conversion. We're at the back. You can tie the dog to that railing there."

"It's raining."

"It's a bloody dog, for Christ's sake. Love rain, dogs."

"How long will we be?"

"It'll be fine. Look. There's even a bit of grass for it to shit on."

Cedric whines a little as she ties him, so she pats his head, looks him in the eyes and tells him to be a good boy, then follows the man down the side of the building. There is a side door with a small sign to one side. The plaque says: *Copacabana*, next to a dancing girl sketched in blue neon. He buzzes the bell and almost immediately the door opens. Cassie sees a large woman with piles of dyed, auburn hair and multi-coloured bangles dangling.

"Well, hello-o!" the woman says, breaking into a huge smile that reveals a gold tooth nestling right at the front, behind the dark red lipstick. "You must be Cassie. Come in, my dear …

"… and thank you, Reggie." She says this with a conspiratorial, richness of tone that tells Cassie they are probably lovers. *Not a pretty thought.*

"Best of luck, darlin'," says the man to Cassie. "You listen to old Sylvia now. She can teach you a thing or two. Play her some reggae, Sylv."

"I'll thank you for less of the *old*, you cheeky bugger."

Cassie feels her warm flesh shiver at being called *darling* by Reg the Raincoat.

"I like a bit of Desmond Dekker meself," says Sylvia as she takes her inside. Cassie pursues her down a fussy

THE LATE SHIFT SPECIALIST

hall. Dozens of small pictures and cartoons cover the flock wallpaper. Things dangle and chime. The smell of burning incense wrestles with a pervasive reek of eucalyptus oil.

"That's it, dear. Come on through."

Cassie follows her through to a dingy room that features a small stage with curtains, lighting equipment and speakers. In front, there is tatty, cinema-style seating for about twenty-five, in three rows.

"We'll start in here," says Sylvia, and they pass through a door to a windowless side room. "Now, let me look at you, properly." She feasts her eyes on Cassie's young body. "What a pretty, little thing you are. Now, you *are* over sixteen, aren't you, dear?"

"I'm eighteen. I told Reg." She couldn't bring herself to call that weasel *Reggie*.

"That doesn't make it true, though, does it dear? Just bring some ID along next time, if you remember. All right?"

Cassie nods and smiles, taking *if you remember* as code for *forget about it*.

"I've laid out a costume for you, dear. Size ten, okay? If you'd like to slip that on for me and, while you're doing that, I'll explain how everything works."

Cassie looks at the bright yellow thong, the white suspender belt and stockings, the low-cut, push-up bra, the glitzy, off-white jacket and pleated mini-skirt, the thigh-length, spangly, cowboy boots. She feels her pulse quicken and she takes a deep breath.

"Don't worry about the outfit, Cassie. We've got others

if that one's not right for you. Now, you and I'll have a little practice session here, with some reggae if you like, and then you can do a little turn on stage for Jazza. He's our impresario, so try and look real sexy for him. And don't hold back. He'll need to see what you've got, if you know what I mean.

"If he likes what he sees, you could be performing next week. We're open Thursday to Sunday, six thirty till two and there's usually six girls doing ten-minute spots with five-minute gaps. So, you can do up to five shows a night, four nights a week. It's a fiver a show, right off the bat. If the lads take to you, that could be a tenner within a couple of months. The best girls are already on that. Not bad, eh?"

Cassie is good at sums. *A hundred quid a week to start, with a chance of doubling that. Wowee!* She'll work out later which time slots she can get away with.

Sylvia sees her struggling to attach the stockings to the suspender belt.

"Here, let me give you a hand with that. They're a bit fiddly but the fellas love 'em."

"What do we do when we're not dancing?"

"That's up to you, as long as you're here for your spot. Some of the girls do a circuit; run round other clubs as well, but you need a car for that. Some just sit around, smoking and talking. No booze mind; it's not that sort of place. One of 'em's learning Spanish, matter of fact. Oh, and then some of that time you might use for private dances. Good money there, if that's to your taste."

"What do you mean?"

"If one of the customers takes a shine to you, he might ask us if you'll dance just for him, in one of the little side-rooms."

"Why?"

"Oooh, you are an innocent, aren't you?"

"Tell me!"

But Sylvia just chuckles quietly.

"Let's stick with the dancing for now, eh? The girls will tell you about the rest. You can put your hand up for private dances or not. Your choice. 'Course, if they keep asking for you, Jazza might want you to give it a try. He's gotta keep the punters happy, after all. Anyway, we'll cross that bridge when we come to it. Alright, darling?"

Cassie is dressed for the part now and pulling on the magnificent boots.

"It suits you a treat, sweetheart. How does it feel?"

"Feels great. Everything fits, more or less."

Cassie goes to a full-length mirror at the end of the room and stands in front of it. She is momentarily startled at the raunchy character staring back at her. She stands with her legs apart and looks straight into her own brown eyes, tugging suggestively on her jacket zipper. She wonders fleetingly if she ought to have spurs, even a whip.

"You could be a natural, dear … Now, what about a stage name? Best not use your real one. Just looking at you there, the name Roxanne came into me head. Dunno why."

"Roxanne," said Cassie, looking at herself sideways in a seductive pose. "Like the Police song? Or Roxy for short, like Roxy Music. Even better, I love it."

"Roxy it is, then. Now, let's see you move, girl."

Sylvia was putting a record on the turntable. After the scratches, *The Israelites* kicked in, tinny and loud. Cassie felt her body crying out to move with it.

"I'm gonna play three records. That'll cover yer ten-minute spot. The first one? Just dance about, nice as you can, smiling, tantalising a bit. Let's see you do that for me.

"That's it. Only loosen up now. Good. You can undo your zipper a bit. Slowly. And smile, darling. Show 'em those lovely teeth of yours. That's better."

I don't want to end up like Bonnie and Clyde, sings Desmond.

"Oooh, oooh-oh, oh-oooh, oo-oooh-oo," sings Cassie.

"It's like I said. You're a natural, Roxy darling."

Sylvia goes back to the turntable.

"Now this one's quite different. More upbeat. D'you know James Brown?"

"My Dad's favourite."

"Then you got a cool Dad, honey. Now really move to this one. Think sexy. Dance for a little bit, then slip the boots off – use the stool there if you want – then dance some more, take off something else. Do it as cool and sexy as you can. Look proud of yourself. Haughty, even. Like they don't deserve you. Because, let me tell you honey, they surely don't. Now, I want you down to thong, stockings and belt by the end of the song. Okay?"

Cassie hears the familiar opening bars of *Papa's Got a Brand New Bag* and she's away, twirling and playing with her jacket zipper. *They'll see there's just a bra underneath.*

"That's good, Roxy. Now the boots, dear."

She perches on the stool and places her right ankle on her left knee with a knowing look. *They'll get a flash of bright yellow thong.* She slowly unzips the boot and slides it off. She stands now and places her left foot on the stool and removes the other boot. And then she is dancing again, in her stockinged feet, sliding a little.

"Now move front of stage, dear, closer to 'em, and take off the jacket. Nice and slow. That's it. Luvverly. And now the skirt. Oooh, they're gonna *love* you, darling."

For the first time, Cassie is looking nervous. Sylvia sees it and turns the music down for a moment.

"It's all right, darling. Take a moment. This is the big one, isn't it, sweetie? I know. The point when you stop being a dancer and start being a stripper. All the girls find it tough, at first. Just remember, you're a beautiful girl and you're beautiful all over. It's your body and you should be proud of it. All of it. And you'll get comfortable soon enough. Probably enjoy it. After all, we all like being admired, don't we? Desired, too. And you *will* be darling. Take it from me. No doubt about that.

"Are we okay now? Ready to carry on?"

Cassie finds a brave grin and Sylvia turns the music back up.

"So, now the bra, dear. Only, tease 'em a bit. Is it coming off or isn't it? Terrific! Then, when you do slip it off, just hold out your arms and let it slide down them. Lovely. Those are very nice, Roxy. Not the biggest, of course, but you're only young. They're absolutely fine."

Cassie wants to hide but she tells herself she can get through this. Sylvia is putting on the final disc.

"Now this one's slow. Sultry. It's good for the sexy bits. You might not recognise it, but it's dead easy to move to. *Jane Firkin' and Surge Forward* we used to call 'em," she titters.

Cassie hears the casual guitar intro, the organ theme cut in and then Jane's breathy voiceover repeating "Je t'aime. Oui, je t'aime."

"This one's four minutes. So, writhe around a bit, looking steamy. That's good. Now run your hands up and down your body, play with your boobs a bit. Yes. But look like you mean it, Roxy. Like it's really turning you on. Like under the bedcovers at home, dear. Yes, that's better. Now spin round, then touch your toes for me and look back at me through your legs … Oh no, dear. Try that again but lose the Heffalump this time. Nice and dainty and spread your legs wider for me. That's more like it. Good. Now have a little dance and then get those stockings off slowly, one by one. Keep looking at me as much as you can. That's it. No, keep the belt on for now. They like that. Now hug yourself a bit, push those boobs together. Gorgeous. And now you can rip that suspender belt off. Just chuck it behind you. A bit of gay abandon, so to speak."

By now, Ms Firkin' is working herself into quite a state.

"Now move forward again and start teasing, big time. They'll be putty in your hands now. Are you going to take that thong off or not? No, not yet, darling. Make 'em suffer. They love it. Look like you want to but you're not sure you should. That's perfect. Now loosen the side ties one by one and hold it there, front and back. Oops!

No, one hand has to go around your bottom to pick up the second tie. That's it."

"Je viens … Aaaaah je viens," moans Jane as the organ grinds on.

"Now, Roxy, start sliding the thong between your legs without showing much. Fabulous. That's very sexy, darling. You're gonna drive them crazy. Now I want you to …"

At that moment, the outside door slams and a man's voice is calling:

"Reg? Sylv? Anyone here?"

Sylvia is moving to the door when it bursts open and a tall, middle-aged, black man confronts her. Angry eyes drill into hers.

"What the *fuck* are you doing with *my* dog?" he shouts, over Jane's fading moans.

"What dog?" says Sylvia.

"*She* brought it," says Reg, who must have seen the man arrive and followed him in.

Only then does the black man register the amateur performer crouching there with one arm covering her breasts and one struggling to hold the yellow thong in place.

"What the *fuck*?"

"She's really good, Jazza. She could be a star."

"She's just a kid, Sylv. What were you thinking?"

"She said she was eighteen."

"She did," said Reg.

"You stay out of this, Reg. And get her some bloody clothes, Sylv."

Jazza growls at Cassie: "You are in *such* trouble, girl."

106

But, with the dressing gown on now, Cassie feels confidence surging back. She is burning with anger, humiliation and resentment.

"*Me* in trouble? Oh, I don't think so. *Jazza*. What was it you told her, way back when? Let's see if I can remember. Oh, yes: 'It's in security, Joan, at the airport. I'll shoot for the six till two slot. We won't see much of each other, but the pay's better and Lord knows we need the money. I'll be the late shift specialist.' Yeah, right.

"What's she gonna think of the job you've *really* been doing for the last four years, you lying toad? What's Mum gonna think when she finds out that her husband, the man she loves and admires, the man she goes arm-in-arm to church with each week, is just a filthy old sleazebag whose immoral earnings come from corrupting vulnerable, young girls?"

Jazza shoots Sylvia a pained look.

"Don't be too hard on him, Roxy darling," she says.

"*Roxy?* Oh, for fuck's sake, Sylv," Jazza howls.

Reg snorts on his cigarette and nearly chokes with suppressed laughter. Jazza throws him a murderous look. Addressing Reg and Sylvia together, finger raised, he hisses: "This never happened, right? A *word* of this gets out, and I'll fire you dunderheads on the spot. Your feet won't touch the fucking ground."

Reg covers his face, but his shoulders are still quaking as Sylvia pulls him away, out of the firing line. Jazza turns to Cassie and his voice softens:

"Get dressed now, girl. We'll talk it through. I've got my reasons and you must have yours, I guess. Maybe

I've been a bit of a tightwad with the pocket money. Dunno. But *we* can sort this out, can't we? Just you and me? Let's take a walk, just like old times …

"… and bring some water for Cedric. The poor little sod's dying of thirst out there."

LEAVING A REVIEW

If you have enjoyed reading my book, it would be wonderful if you could find a minute to complete a short review of *The Late Shift Specialist* on your chosen retailer's website. Thank you!

Alex

THANK YOU

I would encourage all would-be authors to join local writing groups. In my case, they gave me the work ethic, support and critical feedback that enabled my writing to progress. My gratitude and sincere thanks go to the founders and members of Eastcott Writers and Jericho Writers.

Some of the stories in this collection are from aspects of my life, interwoven and overlaid. I would like to thank family members and friends for unwittingly providing the inspiration for these, and the catharsis I found from writing them.

My thanks must also go to:

Two of my friends for their encouragement with my story writing, in particular: former journalist Alexandra ("Sandy") Smithies for her story critiques over rakí and meatballs in Crete and for telling me that my story writing was better than my novels, and my old friend George Schrijver for his growing enthusiasm for everything I write and his earnest and thoughtful feedback.

Swindon Writing for choosing three of these stories to include in their excellent anthology.

Lastly, but by no means least, you for buying and (hopefully) reading this book. I hope you enjoyed it and will find time to leave a review on your retailer's website. If you would like to explore my other writing or sign up for my occasional newsletters, please visit my website at: www.alexdunlevy.com

ABOUT THE AUTHOR

Alex abandoned a career in finance at the age of forty-nine and spent a few years staring at the Mediterranean, contemplating life and loss. Finally, he accepted what his heart had always known. So, he joined a local writing group and he began to write.

Over the next three years, he completed his debut novel, *The Unforgiving Stone.*

This is the first in a series of crime thrillers set on the island of Crete and featuring British protagonist Nick Fisher. The second in the series is expected in spring, 2021.

He has also written this collection of short stories, *The Late Shift Specialist.*

Simultaneously, he has been working on a novel in a very different genre, a black comedy set in the world of corporate finance.

Born in Derbyshire, Alex now divides his time between Wiltshire and Crete.

CONTACT

If you would like to get in touch with Alex, please visit his website: www.alexdunlevy.com where you can join his mailing list, if you wish, and find out about any special offers, or just drop an email to alexdunlevyauthor@gmail.com

He can also be found on Facebook and Twitter.